THE SALTY DOG

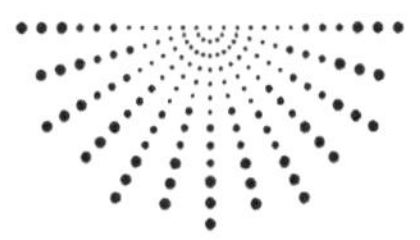

DEBBIE WHITE

CHAPTER ONE

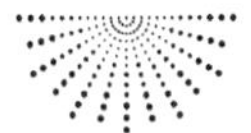

ALONG THE SWEEPING coast sat a cottage above the jagged, rocky coastline. It was so typical of cottages in Bodega Bay with its weather-beaten exterior, wood-shingled roof, and windows from which to view the scenery. It was perfect in every way, and Libby and Luke loved their little cottage by the bay. It was the extreme opposite of their high-rise condominium in San Francisco. Looking back, giving up the noise and crowds was the best thing they'd ever done.

Libby pulled back all the drapes and threw open the French doors. She stood on her porch and gazed across the blue waters before her. She took a deep breath and let it out slowly, taking in the glorious view as she did. The sky was the color of a robin's egg. The wind came from the southwest, bringing with it the smells of fish, algae, and other coastal scents that made living along the coast so wonderful. She slowly walked back into her modest, but comfortable place and proceeded to make her morning coffee. No morning could start without a cup of joe.

Libby poured a cup of the dark brew and as she brought the cup to her lips, she casually looked down at the wagging tail and soft brown eyes that stared back.

"Let's go sit outside and enjoy the morning, Harley."

Libby plopped down in an Adirondack chair and gazed off into the distance. This. This is what had brought them there. Libby reached over and patted Harley on the head.

"He's missing so much, isn't he?" She turned her gaze back toward the glistening water. "I've got some big decisions to make, old boy. None of them are going to be easy. But I just don't think I can handle every-thing anymore. I have the boat to worry about and the café." She quirked her mouth and furrowed her brows as she saw Harley sleeping. He didn't have a care in the world.

"I know. I can't blame you one bit. It's boring and complicated, and well sad frankly. I'd go to sleep if I could, too." Libby smiled.

She drew in another taste of her coffee and reminisced about the day they'd driven to Bodega and looked around. Luke had been convinced this was the best place to move to. At first, she'd dug her heels in. She wasn't moving from San Francisco. Then he'd used his great skill as a storyteller and had begun to romanticize in detail how things would be if she'd just said yes to the move. She'd decided there weren't too many things she wouldn't do for Luke, so with the condition that they would keep the condo – in case things went bad, she'd reluctantly agreed.

That conversation between Luke and Libby seemed so long ago. He'd resigned from his corporate job, they'd pulled out their equity in their condominium, packed up the truck and had driven to Bodega. That had been ten years ago, and she still enjoyed every minute of living with the sea breeze blowing through her hair.

Libby had struggled to adjust to all the hours Luke had spent out on the boat. Anglers' lives involved long hours—from dawn to dusk. They'd discussed what Libby could do to help bring in money to offset the salmon season and to keep busy during his absence. They both agreed something where her office skills could be utilized would be ideal along with her passion of painting and sketching to fall back on. She'd recently sold some of her pieces.

When they had decided to purchase the little dockside café, they'd both known it would require money and time to fix it up. It hadn't operated as a restaurant for a few years. The basic layout had been fine; it had just needed some sprucing up. Luke and Libby had agreed to take a little more money out of the condominium to help purchase the café. They'd come this far, and if they were going to pursue their dreams, they'd have to go all the way. Now, though, running the restaurant and the fishing boat was too much for Libby. She needed help.

The past eight months had been difficult for Libby. She wasn't sure she had what it took. Luke had been the expert commercial angler in the family. It was hard. Work began early in the morning while most people were still snug in their beds. Cold mornings with the wind chill factored in made temperatures feel like they were in the forties on most mornings. Working with frozen shrimp to bait the hooks just added to the discomfort a person felt doing this kind of work.

Salmon fishing north and south of Bodega Bay ran from the first of May to the middle of October. It was chilly out on the water, regardless of the time of year, and the smell of the diesel that powered the boat, mixed with the smell of coffee brewing on the heat source, sometimes was a bit much to stomach.

She had a couple of friends on the dock who helped out, but Sam was the one she relied on the most. Libby had heard a rumor at the café that Sam was looking to purchase his own boat, but she planned a visit to see if she could convince him to work the *Salty Dog* full-time, just like old times.

Luke had loved being out on the water, and he couldn't have fathomed doing anything else. That was Libby's driving force in trying to keep his dream alive. Luke had done everything he could to make it in the commercial fishing world. He and Libby had refinanced their house in the city so they could buy the rig, and they had raided their life savings to keep the business afloat … literally.

Some years, the salmon fishing was more productive than other years. The last two years had been particularly rough. The talk on the docks, however, was that this year would be one of the best. Libby sure hoped they were right. She didn't know how much longer she could survive. Her savings was about gone, and there wasn't any more money in the house to take. Like the rest of the country, property values had suffered significantly in California, leaving their home with negative equity. Fortunately, they had wonderful renters and that was one less burden for Libby.

Bodega Bay at any time of the year was a beautiful

sight, but during the summer it was especially nice, and it brought tourists by the hundreds to see what all the fuss was about. The visitors never left without the desire to return. It had that effect on people. A small seaside town overlooking the cosmic blue that was part of the vast Pacific Ocean had a romantic lure—the same lure that had hooked Luke and Libby many years earlier.

Libby had contracted with a few boat hands who worked on her behalf, but they were not taking it seriously. Libby needed someone who would be loyal and dependable. Be productive—make a living at it, just as Luke had. Sam was the perfect choice. Sam had helped Luke on the fishing boat, and many times Luke had told her he couldn't have done it without him. In fact, Sam had been on the boat with Luke when the accident had occurred.

Sam was an interesting fellow. He originated from Louisiana. His mother was Choctaw Indian and his father was black. He was a very handsome man, with high cheekbones and beautiful bronze skin. His build resembled that of a lumberjack, and his strength was not only appreciated but also needed for the hard work of a fisherman. He'd had a hard life, though, and one day he'd packed up his few possessions and driven to California.

On one of their trips to Bodega, Luke had

befriended Sam when he'd noticed him on the docks doing odd jobs for another fisherman. Luke had wanted to know everything about commercial fishing, and Sam was very knowledgeable. Sam had taken Luke under his wing, and soon he'd become Luke's right-hand man on the *Salty Dog*. Luke would come home and tell her stories that Sam had told him. Some of them were so outlandish that the two of them weren't sure if he was pulling their leg or if it, in fact, they had occurred. As time went on, Libby and Luke had realized the hard life Sam lived gave credibility to his stories, and they'd come to cherish him in more ways than he would ever know. Luke and Libby treasured his friendship.

Since the accident, Libby didn't see much of Sam except when he occasionally came into the café for a bowl of chowder and a cup of steaming hot coffee. She always looked forward to his visits. They didn't talk much, but just seeing Sam gave her some comfort. It had been a while since his last visit. Libby decided she would go to the dock and find him. She wanted to know if there was any truth to the rumor of him getting his own boat, and she wanted to ask him for a big favor.

Libby finished her breakfast and coffee, and then she and Harley walked down to the dock to find Sam.

Libby spotted Sam from a distance. When he looked her way she waved. "Good morning," she yelled. Libby walked toward him smiling. "How are you?"

Sam paused a moment. "I'm doing okay," he said as he hosed off the fish-cleaning area. "How are you?"

Libby cleared her throat. "I could be better. I am having trouble catching the quota, and I need all the fish I can get to take to market." Libby watched as he sprayed the fish guts down the drain.

Sam nodded. "Commercial fishing is hard work, no doubt about it. You have to have the right crew working for you. I could ask around if you'd like," Sam offered.

"Well, that would be great, Sam, but I thought maybe you might be interested in working on the *Salty Dog*." Libby took a step back to get out of his way.

Sam let go of the sprayer and looked up at Libby. He waited a brief second or two before responding, his eyes boring into hers. "Work on the *Salty Dog* full-time?" he said.

"Yes. That would be my preference. If not you, then perhaps you could recommend someone. I haven't had the best luck in securing the most reliable people to help me," she said, looking away.

"I don't know, Libby. I have a lot of work now. Not sure I have time for that."

"Sam, this doesn't have anything to do with the accident does it?

"No, I'm just really busy working for two other guys." He took a broom and began to sweep the water off the dock.

Libby reached out and laid her hand on his arm. "Sam, I don't hold you responsible for the accident. Luke knew the risks of commercial fishing. We all knew the risks. I loved him with all my heart, but he was doing what he wanted to do." Libby sighed.

Sam shrugged his shoulders. "I know. He did love being out on the ocean," he said.

Libby let out another breath. "Just think about it, Sam. That's all I ask. Just please think about it. I need help. I'm going to have to sell the *Salty Dog* if I can't get her out and doing what she is meant to do," Libby said. "I'd just give you the boat, but I...we have too much invested in her. Maybe you'd like to buy her?"

"Buy her. Buy the Salty Dog?" Sam rubbed the scruff on his chin. "I don't know, Libby."

"Luke would have loved you to have her. You were his best friend and..." She lowered her eyes. "I hope you're still my friend, too." She raised her eyes and stared into his.

"Of course you're my friend. I've just been so busy. That's why I haven't been around much."

"I'm glad you're busy. That means you're making a good living. That's important. Especially out here." She looked beyond the dock and watched the seagulls playing in the water.

"I'll stop by the café later this week and give you my answer," Sam said.

They gave each other a hug, and Libby left Sam to finish cleaning the dock.

CHAPTER TWO

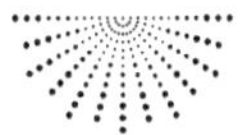

SHE AND HARLEY walked to the café. Avery would be expecting her. With the tourist season in full swing, the café was always busy. Her friend Avery and Avery's husband, Blake, helped Libby run the place. She wouldn't be able to do it without them. They were angels. They'd been by her side from the very beginning.

When Avery and Blake had walked into the café, Libby had instantly liked them. Avery with her dark eyes and flawless complexion, and Blake with sandy blond hair and green eyes, made a beautiful couple. Blake had the surfer look, and Avery had the glamorous model look. Except for her height, she probably could have been a model. Libby figured them both to be about 5'5" or 5'6." She had sat them down, and over coffee, they'd talked in a very casual way. Libby had known before the first cup of coffee was empty that she would hire both of them to help her.

Avery had a charming, yet bold, personality, and Blake possessed a no-nonsense character, so Libby had known the both of them would work well at the café. They both were extroverted, and the restaurant would benefit from their outgoing and confident demeanor.

From the very beginning, Avery and Blake had brought a positive energy to the Seaside Café. They were always happy, and they treated everyone they met warmly. Their kindness was constantly apparent, and their happy-go-lucky attitude brought local customers back repeatedly. Word-of-mouth had customers driving quite a distance and not just for the famous clam chowder and atmosphere. Yes, Avery and Blake had quite a reputation at the Seaside Café. Libby loved having them as her employees, and she definitely enjoyed having them as her friends.

In the evening, after a long day out on the *Salty Dog*, Luke would sit by the fireplace and tell Libby about the day's happenings. Many interesting things took place out in the deep blue ocean. His stories were always fascinating and sometimes scary, too—like the time when the *Salty Dog* had almost collided with a large rock, or when Harley had almost fallen overboard because he hadn't been used to walking around the boat yet and had lost his balance. At the time, all these happenings had been frightening, but because Luke had told her about them after they'd occurred, sometimes they had been even comical. Life on the ocean was like that—never typical, but always exciting. Luke had loved it; in fact, he'd craved it.

There were stories of seals that would jump out of the water as the fishing lines withdrew back to the boat, only to take everything but the fish's head with them back down deep into the ocean. Luke would get upset as this would equate to about a hundred dollars of fish he couldn't take to the market. Luke had also known that what he was witnessing was nature at its finest, the cycle of life playing out right before his very eyes. Those were the risks of being a commercial salmon fisherman.

Libby had always been concerned about his safety, but she'd also known he loved being out on the water with Sam and Harley, his two companions, catching fish with no one to answer to but himself. Libby had known this was his dream, and eventually had gotten used to their life in Bodega, too.

Libby shook off the memories and left Harley at his normal spot outside the café where he greeted the customers. Inside, the morning rush was in full swing. After calling out a greeting to Avery and Blake, she put on her apron and got to work.

JUST AS SAM said he would, he came into the café about a week after Libby's visit to the docks. He ordered his usual, a bowl of clam chowder, a cup of Kona coffee with half-and-half, and a glass of iced tea. Sam sat by the window in his favorite booth and looked out at the inlet. Seagulls flew in the distance, occasionally diving into the water to catch small fish.

Libby came over to the table and sat down. "Hi, Sam, it's nice to see you. How are the coffee and the chowder?" she asked.

"Delicious as always," he responded.

They sat in silence for a few minutes, both of them looking out the window, their minds in different places, but both enjoying the view. Sam broke the silence first.

"Listen, I have thought about what you asked me, Libby. It's going to be hard initially, but we both know it is what Luke would have wanted. So, I am going to take the job," Sam stated.

Libby's face softened. A tiny tear formed on her bottom lid. She blinked it away. "Oh, Sam, that's great news! Thanks so much. Anything I can do to help the process along, just let me know. I am at your disposal," Libby said.

Sam looked steadfastly at Libby. "Well, the boat needs some maintenance done, that's for sure. Whoever it is you contracted with has not been doing a good job about that. I'll need to take her out of the water for a bit, just to make sure she's still seaworthy, clean her up, make sure the lines are in working order, and then we'll be ready for our first voyage," Sam said.

"Whatever is necessary. Thank you, Sam," Libby said as she got up from the booth. She reached over and patted him on the shoulder. "I'm so happy you decided to help me. You are a blessing, pure and simple. Your friendship means the world to me. Thank you."

Sam blushed. Libby walked back toward the kitchen, but not before turning slightly and glancing back at Sam. Libby nodded to him one last time, showing her gratitude that he had accepted her offer.

THE SEASIDE CAFÉ WAS QUAINT, like the rest of

Bodega with gorgeous wood floors distressed from years of being walked on. Strategically placed rustic booths made of lacquered wood afforded great views from the windows facing the inlet. In the middle, there were a few freestanding tables and chairs. On the walls, they'd hung fishing nets, plaques, and other memorabilia representing coastal life, and shelves held huge conch shells and other beach keepsakes. The decorations were very rustic, but in a charming sort of way. The windows on the other two sides of the café offered views of the inlet, the street, and other establishments. Bodega's main street was lined with buildings—it was a shopping and eating paradise for tourists and locals alike. Libby loved her little seaside town. Luke had been right. They'd both learned to love it, and the life they had in San Francisco was all but a fading memory.

Harley had not been the same since Luke's accident. Harley missed Luke dearly, and nothing Libby did seemed to take away the dog's sorrow. She walked him daily, rubbed his belly, and gave him treats. She even let him sleep on the bed now, which Luke had never allowed him do. She wanted to bring life back to the old boy, but nothing seemed to work. She wouldn't give up, though. She adored Harley, and it was important for them to be close again. Harley was all Libby had right now, besides the café and her friends. Avery and Blake went home together every night. Libby just had Harley.

After another long shift at the Seaside Café, Libby and Harley walked home. The house seemed so quiet and empty. She walked over to the French doors and opened them, letting the night breeze blow through. Harley went out onto the balcony to lie down while Libby turned on the television. She really wasn't in the mood to watch television. It seemed the news always portrayed the bad things happening in the world. Sitcoms weren't funny to her, and she definitely was not in the mood for romance. She flipped through the channels and then, as most nights, turned the television off. She walked over to the bookcase and took out the photo album.

Libby sat out on the balcony with Harley and looked at the pictures. It seemed so surreal to not have Luke here to enjoy the life they had made. She flipped through pictures of them when they were dating, of their wedding, before and after their condominium remodel in the city, of their puppy Harley, and of course, of the *Salty Dog*. Tears began to form around Libby's bottom eyelids. She quietly closed the album and stared out at the black, massive sky and the sea before her. Except for a few twinkling lights of night boats, everything appeared very obscure and ominous.

"C'mon, Harley, let's call it a night," Libby said.

The next few days were busy for Sam and Libby both. Sam pulled the *Salty Dog* out of the water and performed some badly needed maintenance. He scraped off the barnacles that had taken up residence on the bottom and put a fresh coat of paint on to make her shiny and new, and then the *Salty Dog* was almost ready for the water. Sam changed the engine oil and checked all the pulleys and lines, and after only a couple of weeks, the *Salty Dog* was back out on the sea trolling for salmon.

Bodega Bay had a deep-rooted history that began with the Miwok Native Americans who had lived on its shores. A shallow, rocky inlet of the Pacific, the Spanish-Peruvian explorers of the Spanish Navy had anchored their ships in the bay. Famous movies such as Alfred Hitchcock's *The Birds* and a 1980 horror film titled *The Fog* had put Bodega on the map because they both featured the town. The fog was a real thing for Bodega. It was so thick on many mornings that it made driving dangerous. The visibility was literally only inches. The *Salty Dog* would travel out to deeper waters and sometimes motor through the thick fog. It was an eerie feeling for Libby, but Luke had liked the mystery the fog represented. She would often imagine that there were spirits out with them, and not being able to see beyond her own nose was sometimes just too terrifying to her. She was always happy when she could see daylight peek through the puffy clouds of fog. She could rest easy then.

Libby had been thankful she hadn't needed to go out salmon fishing very often with Luke. She did like to take boat rides, though, and when they could, they'd packed some lunch, and the two of them, along with Harley, had motored out and enjoyed the beautiful scenery. Libby would take her sketch pad and watercolors and record the beautiful images on paper. She'd even displayed a few in the café and at a local gift store. She'd had sold a few, too, but mostly she sketched for fun.

Luke and Libby had also christened the boat a few times with lovemaking. Something about being out on the water provided the ever-essential environment for passion. Luke had been a great kisser, and it had never taken much for Libby to melt into his arms and succumb to his every desire. Her desire, too, for that matter. Luke had found very private little coves where they could anchor the boat. After a full day out on the ship, sketching, and romancing, they'd often worked up quite an appetite. They'd often stopped in at the

Seaside Café to see how Avery and Blake were doing, too.

Libby hadn't known it—no one could have—but the last time they'd gone boating would turn out to be the last time ever for them.

CHAPTER THREE

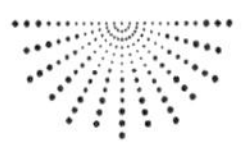

LIBBY REMEMBERED the day as if it was just yesterday. She'd looked up to see the Coast Guard personnel and local sheriff standing in the doorway to the café, and Sam with Harley by his side. It all had seemed so surreal, the presence of these strangers, and her friends standing in the doorway of the café. She'd immediately known it wasn't good news. She had been able to tell by the look on their faces. Sam appeared to have been crying; the look on the men's faces had told the whole story. Even Harley had hung his head low to the ground. Libby had started shaking as she walked toward them, looking for some sign that it wasn't as bad as it appeared, but knowing deep down that it was.

Libby recalled Sam hugging her, consoling her, but most of all, she remembered crying uncontrollably.

Beyond that, the day was a blur. Those days sometimes felt just like yesterday, and sometimes they seemed far removed. It was how Libby functioned from day to day. That his body was never retrieved from the icy cold waters of Bodega was the hardest part for Libby. It was hard for her to have the closure necessary to move on.

Avery had helped Libby organize a memorial for Luke. He had many friends within the commercial fishing industry and as the owner of the Seaside Café. The community liked Luke, and it helped Libby having them present to show respect for her husband. It had meant a lot to her. A very solemn day, one that would remain forever etched in her mind.

Now that Sam was running the *Salty Dog* again, Libby had faith that everything would be okay. Luke would see to it.

The *Salty Dog* was trolling for salmon again, just like old times, and being very productive. With Sam as the captain, along with the crew he had hired, the daily catch was exceeding their expectations.

The Seaside Café was also doing great. Libby felt, for the first time in over a year, that just maybe things were looking up. She smiled as she thought of Luke smiling down on her. "*Love you, Luke,*" she whispered.

Libby looked up when Blake announced he needed to run to the fish market to get some clams.

"I'm going to take some money from the petty cash drawer," he said. Libby, glad for the interruption, told him to take a little extra for some shrimp. "Tell Mr. Larry I said hi, and I will be making a trip down there soon. I'm in the mood for some fresh halibut," she added.

"You got it," Blake said as he opened the cash drawer. He scribbled his name on a voucher with the day's date and the reason for purchase and put it back in the drawer. Libby ran a tight ship with the finances. She recognized firsthand that good record-keeping was essential for running a good business, and the staff knew it.

"I'll be back soon," he said as he went out the door, causing the wind chime to sound.

Hearing the wind chime brought back great memories for Libby. It had been on one of their trips along the coast, looking for a boat and a new place to hang their hat, that they'd come upon a cute little gift store. They'd wanted to stretch their legs and get a bite to eat, and the sign displayed out front had said Best Chowder Ever. The owner of the little chowder stand had been very sweet and knowledgeable about the area. Old Mr. Parker, as the locals affectionately had known him, had proceeded to tell Libby and Luke about the history of the town. All the while, they'd been eating truly one of the best chowders they'd ever had. In fact, Mr. Parker had been the one who'd given Libby the recipe for the chowder she now served at the Seaside Café.

After having enjoyed the wonderful conversation with Mr. Parker and eating his excellent chowder, Libby had decided to look around the little gift store. The shop had really been just an oversized canopy with rows of beach stuff. Through their discussion with Mr. Parker, Libby had found out that he left it up all summer long. She had walked up and down, looking at the various things he had, but she'd kept returning to a beautiful wind chime made of shells and little metal doodads hanging from fishing line. It was somewhat rustic looking, but had a charm about it, too. Later she would discover that the metal doodads were weights for fishing lines. She'd loved the little strange-looking wind chime. She had given Mr. Parker the eight dollars he was asking, and then Luke and she had set off on another journey along the coast. It had been somewhat of a coincidence, maybe, or ironic at best, but Luke and Libby had ended up in the same town with Mr. Parker and his little store and chowder stand. The wind chime meant that much more to Libby, knowing that Luke and Mr. Parker were no longer with them.

The café was always busy, so Libby often would pitch in and clean off tables. Avery and Libby did whatever was necessary, including keeping the place clean and the restrooms stocked with toilet paper. Blake, on the other hand, would be in the kitchen cooking up a storm. The girls relied on his cooking skills. Luke and Libby had decided early on that the café would have a small menu. Their philosophy: make a limited menu, but make it great. And great it was. Old Mr. Parker's chowder, fried clams, fish sandwiches, French fries, shrimp made a few ways, and for the children, grilled cheese and the standard burger.

The little local paper had written a five-star review about the Seaside Café, and that helped even more. Whenever tourists came into town, the locals always directed them to the café for lunch. They only served lunch and dinner. They had an extensive wine selection, featuring Napa and Sonoma wines, and they also had a nice little dessert menu thanks to a local baker. Cheesecake was one of the favorites, but during apple and peach season, the cobbler was in high demand.

Libby worked long hours with very little time off. Avery and Blake worked just as hard. It was difficult to give anyone time off, especially during the tourist season. Libby would insist that they take at least one day off each week. Libby loved the distraction that work offered. She didn't particularly like being alone, but she was used to it. However, surrounding herself with laughter from the locals beat sitting home and looking at four walls.

Libby had just finished clearing a table and was walking toward the bussing station to drop off the dirty silverware and plates when she looked up and saw a very handsome man standing in the doorway. Libby looked around the dining room to see if anyone was flagging him down as a possible lunch date. She didn't see any such movement, so she walked up to him with a menu in her hand and asked, "Lunch for one?"

"Yes, please."

Libby smiled. His eyes sparkled and seemed to draw her in.

She seated him, gave him the menu, and asked if she could get him a drink.

He replied, "Just water, please."

Libby walked over to the beverage bar and grabbed a pitcher of ice water. She walked back over to his table and filled his glass. She said to him as she was pouring, "Do you need a few more minutes, or do you know what you'd like to eat?"

"Well, I heard you all serve the best clam chowder for miles around. Is that right?" he queried as he smiled up from the menu. His eyes pierced through hers causing her heart to beat faster. "Well, actually, I've been told that. I don't want to sound conceited or anything …" she said modestly, feeling her cheeks flush as she stared at his large hands. She noticed he didn't wear a ring.

"I'll take one bowl of chowder with bacon crumbled on the top," he said. "Oh, and shredded cheddar; I hear that really makes the difference," he added as he handed Libby back the menu.

"A bowl of chowder with all the toppings, coming right up," she said as she smiled at him.

Libby took the order into the kitchen for Blake to serve up the chowder. They kept a huge kettle of that stuff going all day long since it was one of the most requested items on their menu. When workers came in on their lunch break, it was a quick, easy meal to get back out to them.

Libby arranged the bowl with crackers on a tray and began to go back out to the dining area with it, but first she cleared her throat. "After I leave, take a look at the guy sitting at table #5," she whispered to Avery as she breezed by her.

Libby approached his table. She sat the steaming bowl in front of him, laying the soup spoon next to it.

"Wow, does this ever look and smell good!" he said as he looked up at her. His eyes twinkled like little stars dancing against a dark blue sky, his teeth a sparkling white.

"I hope you enjoy it. If you need anything else just ask."

"I will. Thank you," he said.

Libby made her way to the kitchen, and just in time to see a smidgeon of Avery backing away from the door.

"I've never seen him in here before. He must be just traveling through," Avery said.

"I don't know. He said he'd heard about us. He's not our typical customer, that's for sure."

"He's a hottie," Avery said.

"Oh there's the chime. Another customer." Libby said.

Libby walked by table five as she seated the next set of patrons. She couldn't help but look at the man as she walked by. He was very handsome, or as Avery had announced, a hottie.

Libby went over to the serving area where they kept pitchers of water and extra utensils. She was trembling, and she could feel her heart racing a mile a minute. This guy sparked something in her that she hadn't felt in a long time. Not since Luke had she felt anything remotely like this, and the pull to stay in the dining room was strong. She didn't want to leave.

She grabbed a dishrag and headed toward a recently vacated table and began clearing dishes. As much as she tried to concentrate on the job at hand, Libby found herself peering his way to see what he was doing, which was eating his soup, drinking his water, and gazing out the window at the beautiful scenery.

Because the café was small, Libby often ran the cash register, too. Everyone pitched in where needed. When it was time for him to pay his bill, Libby found herself ringing him up. He paid with cash, and when Libby gave him his change, he walked back over to his table and threw a couple of dollars onto it. As he walked out, he glanced back over at her, smiled, and said, "Thanks for lunch. I'll be back." As the door opened and then closed, the memories of the wind chime once more played for Libby.

CHAPTER FOUR

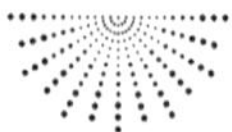

Libby had a hard time concentrating the rest of the day. She kept busy, bussing tables and helping out in the kitchen, but when it was time to lock up for the evening, she was kind of glad. She felt mentally worn out, as well as physically. Avery and Blake told Libby they would finish cleaning so she and Harley could call it a night. Libby didn't argue. She called Harley to come to her, and they walked home in silence.

Harley accompanied Libby just about everywhere she went. He was a great dog. He listened well, and Luke had trained him in many commands. The locals loved that Harley came to work with her. He would lie outside on the front porch and greet the customers as they came in and looked forward to a pat on the head when they left.

Libby unlocked the front door to the house, and Harley trotted in checking out the place to make sure there were no intruders. At least, that's what Libby told herself. She felt he was always looking out for her, and Luke was making sure of that. She turned on the lights in the house and, as usual, drew open the curtains and opened up the French doors for some fresh air. She quickly looked through the day's mail, throwing all the junk away.

Libby turned on the television to catch the nightly news. She was not really paying that much attention as she searched the net on her tablet when something she heard piqued her interest. The local reporter was telling the viewers that a business tycoon was in the area looking to start a new venture. Libby looked up just in time to see the same man she'd served lunch to in her café earlier that day. She quickly sat down on the edge of the couch to watch the rest of the segment. When it was over, she picked up the phone.

"Apparently he is a winery owner and was scouting out areas where he could open a tasting room."

Avery laughed. "Well I guess some areas of California are flooded with them, so why not come out to the coast," she said.

"He told the reporter that he found Bodega to be

charming, and it was on his short list of places," Libby said.

"Well good luck on finding a place is all I'm gonna say," Avery added.

"Well, I just thought you'd be interested in our mystery guy."

"Me interested? Did you see the way he looked at you? Blake and I could feel the heat all the way in the kitchen, and it wasn't coming from our big pot of grits."

Libby held the phone away from her ear and smiled. She cleared her throat. "Yeah, something definitely was happening between us. But…"

"But what?"

"I don't know, Avery. It feels weird."

"Weird because of Luke?"

Libby sighed. "Partly. It's just I haven't flirted or dated in so long, I'm not sure if I even know what to do."

"First of all, get it out of your head right now any stupid ideas you have that Luke wouldn't want you to be happy. I know he would. He loved you that much, Libby. Secondly. If it feels hot, it is!" Avery snorted into the phone. "Someone call a fireman, we have a blaze to put out," she said, laughing so hard she started coughing.

"Avery. Are you all right? Does Blake need to do CPR on you?"

"Girl, see you tomorrow," she said still laughing. "I hope your hot new man comes in. Maybe you can get his number this time."

"Avery!" Libby disconnected the call and turned off the television, then she called Harley in from one of his favorite spots out on the porch. She locked up, turned off the lights, and went to her room with Harley following close behind. He plopped down on his large, down-filled dog bed, moaning a little as he got comfortable. Libby let out a little laugh. "It sucks to get old, doesn't it?"

Libby proceeded to get ready for bed, first brushing her teeth, then her hair. She started to apply her night cream when she realized Harley was eyeballing her. Libby reached down and patted him on the head. He let out one last little moan and then stretched out.

"Good night, boy. I know. Another day and night without him."

Libby pulled down the covers and slid in. She reached for the light switch, turning off the bedside light. Snuggling deep under the covers, Libby pulled them up to her neck and lay there listening to the quietness of the house. She again thought about the handsome man who'd visited the café and the news report she had seen on television. She thought about Sam, too, and realized that soon he would be getting up to take the *Salty Dog* out while the rest of the world slept. Exhausted from her busy day, Libby closed her eyes and soon drifted off to sleep.

The next morning, Libby felt refreshed and knew she would be able to take on anything, expected or otherwise. She had going down to the docks to see Sam on her agenda, so she showered, and while the coffee was brewing, she took Harley out for his morning walk.

The air was so fresh in Bodega. It was always a little chilly on the coast, but when summer came and the heat index inland grew unbearable, people would drive out to Bodega to get much-needed relief from the heat. Libby and Luke used to drive to Sonoma and Napa Counties when they wanted heat. They'd both loved the backroads of the beautiful countryside, and wine tasting was something they'd both liked to do. Many of the wineries had beautiful picnic areas where you could wine and dine as you took in the beautiful surroundings and experience Mother Nature at her best. Both Luke and Libby had appreciated the environment. It really was hard to beat the geography of the wine country.

As Libby walked Harley, she reminisced about one of the times they'd driven to Napa. The night before, they'd mapped out which wineries they would visit.

They'd set out mid-morning and had driven the hour or so to get to the first winery. After a couple of samples, they'd purchased cheese, crackers, and other snack items from a nearby deli and had filled their tummies as they'd sipped some more wine. The sun's warmth and the sky's intense blue had made the day perfect. Libby missed those times.

Libby quickly stopped daydreaming when Harley started barking. She looked up just in time to see Sam. She waved as she began to walk toward him. Harley was tugging at the leash, anxious to say hello.

"Good morning, Sam," Libby said as she struggled to keep Harley under control.

"Good morning to you," he said as he leaned over and gave Harley a nice pat on the head and rubbed him under his ears.

"This is kind of ironic, us meeting this morning. I was planning on coming down to the docks to see you later today," Libby said.

"Oh?" Sam said with a surprised look on his face. "Is everything okay?"

"Yes. I just wanted to touch base with you and see how things are going on the boat," she said as she swept the hair away from her face.

"Things are going well. In fact, the crew I hired has turned out to be a great bunch. They get in there and actually work hard. I think you'll be impressed with this week's numbers," he added.

"That's great, Sam. Thanks again for all your hard work. Well, guess I better get back to the house and get ready for work. The café has been crazy busy these past few weeks. Aren't you due to come in for a bowl of chowder?"

"I can taste it now. Look for me sometime this week," he replied giving Libby a quick nod before he turned back towards the docks.

"Looking forward to it," she called out to him as they both went their separate ways.

"C'mon, Harley, we need to get back and finish getting ready for work," Libby said, gently tugging on Harley's leash.

Back at the house, Libby poured herself a cup of coffee and quickly ran through the things she would need to attend to at the café. She thought about the news story she had seen the night before regarding the winery owner and wondered if he would make another appearance at the café today. Most likely not; he had just been there. However, it would be nice to see him again, she thought.

Down at the café, things were already in full swing with a busy lunch crowd. Blake was hard at work in the kitchen. Libby took in a deep breath through her nostrils. The simmering chowder and baked cornbread tricked her senses into thinking it was lunch time. The cornbread was a new menu item for them. They usually served sourdough bread slices. However, a local regular customer had suggested that cornbread would go well with the chowder. Libby aimed to please, so she said they would try it. Blake researched recipes online and found one that had a touch of honey in it. It was moist and delicious—two key requirements for good cornbread.

Avery was busy as usual, brewing coffee, steeping tea bags for iced tea, and filling all the soda machines with new pressurized bottles. Libby pitched in and starting filling pitchers with ice and water. She sliced some cucumbers to float in the water pitchers. It added a crisp, clean taste to tap water. The customers really liked it, too. Libby had gotten the idea from a local sushi restaurant she and Luke had visited regularly. They both had commented on how much they enjoyed drinking the water with the cucumber floating among the ice cubes.

The café was buzzing with all the gossip regarding the possible wine tasting shop. Libby couldn't help but overhear some of the scuttlebutt. Most people were excited about the new business prospect. Anything to attract tourists, Bodega would be for. The town thrived on tourism. Libby wondered what areas of town he was considering for his new shop. She decided she'd ask him—if he ever came back into the café, that is.

"Ten minutes until crazy," Libby yelled back to the kitchen."

Avery swung open the kitchen door. "We're ready. Unlock the door." She laughed.

Lunch time was always hectic at the café.

Libby startled when she heard the wind chime. She looked up and saw the handsome man from yesterday. She couldn't help but wonder if this was a sign. She took a menu off the counter and approached him.

"Back again so soon?" she said, smiling up at him.

"Yes. I couldn't stop thinking about the clam chowder, among other things," he said, his gaze sweeping her features and heating her skin.

Rubbing the back of her neck, Libby shifted her weight from one foot to the other. "Well, follow me." Libby clasped her hands and rocked back on her feet before leading the way to the same little table he had sat at the day before.

She started to leave the menu with him, but he pushed it aside and said, "I'll have the same as yesterday. And I was wondering if you'd care to join me?"

Libby widened her eyes. "Join you?"

The man nodded.

"I would …" She looked at the other patrons. "But I'm working right now."

"Aren't you the owner?"

She raised her brows. "Yes. How'd you know that?"

"This is a small town," he chuckled.

Libby nodded. "True."

She turned away from him. "Coming up. Chowder with all the toppings," she bellowed as she walked into the kitchen. Her fingers trembled, then her stomach began to tighten and pull. She felt a wave of nausea and took a couple of deep breaths to ward it off. It seemed to work. She wiped the little drops of perspiration that dampened her brows.

Avery looked up at Libby as she entered the kitchen. "What's the matter, Libby?

Libby began fanning her pink, flushed face. "Nothing."

Avery tossed diced potatoes into a large covered dish. "Are you sure? What is going on with you, Libby?" Avery asked.

Libby, not sure how to respond, finally said, "It's nothing."

Avery narrowed her eyes. She crossed over to the kitchen door, opened it a little, and peered around it. She pulled the door shut quickly, then turned back to Libby. "Nothing, huh? It's just the winery owner again.

Listen, you go wait on him and take all the time you need."

Libby couldn't explain the feelings she was having for this man. Someone she'd really just met, but she definitely was attracted to him. Exasperated, she carried his regular order over to the table and set it down.

"This looks and smells delicious. I can tell your chef makes the same recipe every time. I love that," the man said.

"We've been making it for a while now. Blake is the man in the kitchen, for sure," Libby said with some spunk in her voice. "Would you like anything else?"

"This will do for now. Unless you changed your mind and can join me?"

"I'm Libby," she blurted.

"Nice to meet you, Libby." He held out his hand. "My name is Jackson. Jackson Keys."

"Nice to meet you." She paused, then added, "I saw you on the news last night, and I know why you're here. You're scouting out places for a winery."

He pursed his lips tightly. "Not really a winery. I have that. I'm looking for a wine tasting room where I can showcase my wines."

Libby smiled. "I'll have to check out your winery

sometime. Maybe I've already been before. My husband—" Libby stopped, not finishing the statement.

Jackson's eyes dropped to her hand. Her left hand. She'd removed her wedding ring, but now wore it on a chain around her neck.

"My husband died in a terrible accident."

"I'm sorry for your loss."

Not sure what else to say, she said, "Well, I'll let you get back to your lunch."

Jackson lowered his chin and picked up the spoon. "I'd really like to pick your brain sometime about the area. As a businesswoman, you must have some ideas of where I might be able to set up a wine tasting room. Everyone I ask here in town tells me to ask you. Everyone's been very impressed with how you turned this café around."

Libby tilted her head. She'd never really thought of all her hard work as impressive. She just did what she knew she had to do.

"Okay. Maybe," Libby said, and then went back to the kitchen to catch her breath. She couldn't believe how she was behaving—like some schoolgirl.

"So, what did he say?" Avery asked as she whipped the fresh cream for homemade topping. The cheesecake they served was delicious with just a dollop and fresh strawberries as garnish—when they were in season.

Libby went to the refrigerator to see if there were any strawberries to slice. She took the large green basket from the fridge and rinsed off the berries. She pulled out a cutting board and proceeded to slice them.

"He said that the locals told him to come here and talk to me."

"Talk to you about what?"

Libby shrugged. "About finding a location for his wine tasting room. I guess the locals think I have all the answers since I took the café from nothing to this," Libby gestured with her head the kitchen area and beyond.

"He's flirting with me, too." Libby blurted.

"Good." Avery said matter of fact.

Libby sighed. "I flirted back, too. I think."

"Good!" Avery said.

"He wants to ask me for some advice. It sounded like a date, but maybe it isn't." Libby sliced the strawberries with the knife. "Man, am I out of practice."

"Go for it. Date. Advice. Whatever he wants to call it. You go for it." Avery winked.

The chimes on the door rang. Libby dried her hands on her apron and walked out of the kitchen.

Sam was standing there. "Hi! I'm glad you decided to come by so soon," Libby said cheerfully.

"I wanted to discuss a few things with you and felt it couldn't wait any longer. I know you're so busy with the café, and all," he added. "I just really need to talk to you."

Libby looked at him oddly. She could tell something was truly bothering him, something so powerful that he hardly could look her in the eyes. "Let's sit down over here," she said as she led him to a vacant table.

"Okay," he said as he followed her.

They both sat down at about the same time. Libby looked at Sam, waiting for some sign that he was about to start talking. The silence was killing her. Everything she came up with was bad. She wanted to yell, "What's the matter?" Instead, she just sat there in silence, too. After what seemed like several minutes, Libby finally broke the silence. Looking directly at Sam, Libby said, "You're frightening me. What's wrong?"

"I don't know if this is even the right place to talk about this," Sam replied in a very low voice. "We've never really talked about it … the accident."

"Sam, we've been through this before. I told you, I do not hold you responsible in any way," she said meaningfully. "It was an accident," she added as she dropped her head down, saddened by the conversation.

"It happened all so fast. I wasn't really paying attention … I think I could have—"

"Listen," Libby interrupted him before he could go on, "You have to stop doing this … to me … to you … we can't keep rehashing the what-ifs, Sam," she said.

"You've never asked me about that day. Don't you need to hear it for closure? Cuz I need to tell you so that I can move on. That's what's missing here."

Libby tried to relax her shoulders. "I guess I didn't want to hear it because then I'd know. But you're right."

"It started out as such a beautiful day. We had the radio playing an oldies station, and Harley had been lying in the bow of the boat. I was on the port side checking lines, and Luke was on the starboard side doing the same. Luke yelled out to me that a school of dolphins was swimming and showing off on the starboard side of the boat. I quickly made it over there just in time to see them. It was always a beautiful sight, no matter how many times we saw it.

"It had been a great day. We'd anticipated an extraordinary windup, catching our limit of salmon. Line after line, we pulled in some of the largest salmon out there. We were sure to see an enormous profit after that day's catch, and that made us both happy."

Libby nodded.

"We'd spent several extra hours out, longer than we'd been out before. Time had gotten away from us and before we realized it, it was dusk and the waves were getting a bit rough. A storm had been brewing, and it took us by surprise. The *Salty Dog* had been rocking and rolling with the waves when Luke lost his balance and slipped, hitting his head on the hydraulic pulley system and falling overboard. I was too late. I couldn't save him." Sam lowered his eyes.

Libby reached out and touched his hand. Sam had been through as much as she had. He was a dear friend, and his loss was nearly as deep as hers.

Libby nodded her head and smiled a half smile. "He was the love of my life, Sam. You were his best friend. I know you did everything you could. It's not your fault. I'm just thankful the sea didn't claim your life, too.

This time, Sam nodded.

Libby stiffened her shoulders. "How about a piece of cheesecake?" She pulled back her chair.

Sam smiled.

"With or without strawberries?"

"With," he replied.

"I'll be right back."

Libby set the cheesecake down in front of him and then took her seat opposite him. "Listen, Sam. I know it's out of your comfort zone…working on the boat, and I totally understand, but we've both grieved for Luke, and now, we must go on living. That's what he would want. If it's too much, you working on the *Salty Dog*, just let me know."

"I see the spot—the dried blood where he fell and hit his head," he said, lowering his eyes to the slice of creamy dessert.

Libby furrowed her brows. "I know. That's why I've avoided going on the boat. I know my eyes will go to that spot, too. Maybe we should refinish the planks?"

"It's no use. I'll always know where that spot is no matter if we scrub it clean, refinish it, or what have you. It's etched into my brain."

Libby nodded. "I know," she whispered. "What can we do but move on? He wants us to do that, I know he does," Libby said desperately.

Libby reached over and patted Sam on the hand. It would be the last time the two of them ever spoke about the accident again. They both got the closure they needed. From that day forward, Sam and Libby discussed salmon, how many pounds were caught, the price per pound, and how the *Salty Dog* was operating. Occasionally, Libby would go out on a salmon run. Although it wasn't her thing, she knew it meant a lot to Sam.

Libby had almost forgotten about the handsome man after the deep discussion that took place with Sam. She casually crossed over to his table to see if he needed anything else. "I think I'm ready for the bill," he said, smiling up at Libby.

As if on cue, her heart started pounding, her palms became sweaty, and she had a difficult time speaking. She tore his check out of her order pad and laid it on the table. Finally, she found a little strength and managed to form words. "Whenever you're ready, I'll be your cashier," she said and turned away.

The guy reached out and lightly held her wrist. Libby spun around to face him, startled by his behavior. When their eyes met, Libby felt like he was looking deep into her soul. Finally, he spoke. "I was being serious about meeting with you. Could you take some time for a business lunch?"

She began to sputter out a few words, then took in a deep breath and regrouped. "Yes, I can do that. When would you like to meet?"

"I live a couple of hours away, but I love the drive." He removed a business card from his wallet and handed it to her. She looked it over then stuck it in her apron pocket. He reached back into his wallet retrieving a ten-dollar bill tossing it on the food receipt. Libby stepped back so he could exit the table.

As he made his way toward the door, Libby got a whiff of his cologne. It lingered in the air tantalizing her senses.

"I'll call you soon," she said.

"Goodbye," he said as he opened the door to the café and walked out.

Libby stood in silence as she watched him leave. Not sure what had just happened, she returned to the kitchen in a daze.

"Hey, Libby, can you peel some potatoes for me?" Avery asked.

"Sure," Libby replied as she took a paring knife from the knife block on the counter. Libby began to peel the potatoes as Avery watched. When Libby sensed that Avery was watching her in a peculiar way, she gave her a dirty look.

Avery responded with, "What?"

Libby just shook her head. "Why are you staring at me?" Libby raised her brows.

"I'm not staring at you. I'm just trying to figure out what's up with that handsome customer—the one who has come in two days in a row!" Avery exclaimed.

Libby pulled out the big stainless steel strainer from the cabinet and placed it in the sink. She took the peeled potatoes, put them in the strainer, and ran cold water over them to rinse them off before dicing them.

"Libby! I know you want to tell me." Avery sang out.

Libby turned on the sprayer and while in the midst of washing the spuds she decided to have a bit of fun lightly spraying Avery in the face with the water. Avery laughed as she reached out to grab the sprayer from Libby's hand.

Blake was at the stove stirring the clam chowder, grilling a hamburger patty, and making fries when he heard the commotion. He looked up for a brief moment and smiled as he flipped the burger.

"We don't need any accidents in the kitchen," he quipped as he continued to cook. Libby frowned; Avery stuck her tongue out at him. In the end, Avery pulled out some white bar towels to soak up the water while Libby drained the potatoes and put them in the fridge.

CHAPTER FIVE

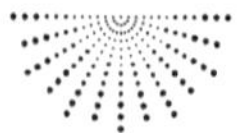

BUSINESS WAS PICKING up big time, and Libby realized she would have to hire some more workers before Blake and Avery walked out on her for being exhausted. Although a small town, Bodega boasted several stores and restaurants up and down the coastline. However, when the regulars who frequented the café heard she was hiring, word of mouth brought all several applicants in. If the locals didn't know them, Avery or Blake knew them because they'd lived here their whole lives.

Hunter, the star quarterback for the high school and very popular with the young ladies, soon had the café full of giggling young girls occupying tables.

The second young person she hired was Anthony. Anthony was one of eight children. His parents were immigrants from Mexico. Libby knew who they were;

they had their own shrimp boat in town. Tony, as he preferred to be called, didn't tolerate being out on the boat very well, because he had severe seasickness. Still wanting to earn money to help the family, he'd asked permission to seek other employment. Libby was sad for him and his situation, but happy for her and the café. Tony had not only some cooking experience, but he also spoke Spanish fluently, which would be good for the Seaside. During the interview, Libby also learned that Tony was very active in his church, and he was very pragmatic—something not seen too often in a young man of his age. Libby felt that the combination of the two boys would be great for the Seaside Café.

The last person hired was a single woman about sixty-five years old or so. Some folks would label her as a senior citizen, but Libby saw her as a wealth of experience, dedication, and loyalty all rolled into one. She had lots of experience waiting tables. She'd found it necessary to go back to work after she'd retired from the school district. She couldn't make ends meet on her meager pension. It was somewhat ironic that Tony and Hunter had, at one time, both had her as a teacher. Libby felt that her skills would be a great asset for the Seaside, and in return, she would compensate Mrs. Johnson justly. Mrs. Johnson was jovial and her carefree attitude seemed to fit the cafe.

Libby was excited about her new employees. She knew that to be on the safe side, they would need one more employee—someone to help Blake with the cooking. After a few days and no more applicants from word of mouth, she placed a three-by-five-inch card at the post office. "Help wanted. Experienced front line cook. Must be able to work in a fast-paced kitchen. Small, standardized menu. Inquire at the Seaside Café. Ask for Libby."

Libby was busy cleaning off tables when she heard the wind chime. She looked up and saw a young man walk into the café. He had shoulder-length brown hair, brown eyes, and average-looking features. He was dressed in jeans, a T-shirt, and tennis shoes. He had a backpack slung over his shoulder, and in his right hand, he held the three-by-five-inch card. She immediately noticed a warm smile. His eyes seemed to twinkle and on second glance, Libby thought his brown eyes were warm and inviting.

"Are you here for the cook position?" she asked the man.

"Yes, I am," he responded.

Libby extended her hand to the stranger. "My name is Libby."

"Nice to meet you. My name is Marshall."

Libby looked around the room, her eyes settling on

an empty booth in the back of the café. "Let's go over here," she said as she walked toward the booth. He waited for her to sit first, and then he sat across from her. He laid his backpack on the bench. Libby cleared her throat. "What kind of cooking experience do you have?"

"I've worked with lots of fast food-type restaurants from Maine to California and everywhere in between," he said slowly and clearly.

"Oh, I see. Hamburgers and the like?" she asked.

He straightened his shoulders and raised his left brow. "I've flipped a few burgers in my time." They both chuckled about that. Marshall continued with his resume. "I've worked in lots of different venues—Mexican, Chinese, and even a sandwich shop," he said. There was no doubt this guy had confidence. Libby liked that about him.

"Have you ever worked in a seafood restaurant?"

"Not a seafood restaurant, specifically, but I have worked in restaurants that offered shrimp and other seafood on their menus," he added.

Libby nodded. "Let me tell you a little about the Seaside," Libby said. "We mostly cater to locals; however, we are actually seeing an influx of tourists lately. This café has only been in operation for about five years. We are really expanding our base of clients and returning travelers. Our menu is small. We're best known for our delicious clam chowder. We also serve fried fish, shrimp, and a few other items—and we are looking to introduce some "new" standards as well." Marshall nodded his head. "What experience and suggestions can you bring to our little café?" Libby asked openly.

"Well, I love to cook. I don't want to brag, but I've been told that I make a delicious shrimp scampi and shrimp tacos. I also like to make macaroni and cheese with lobster."

Libby licked her lips. "Wow, those items sound great." Libby glanced down to the one-page application.

"I see you don't have a permanent address." She looked up at him.

"I'm looking for a place. Right now, I live in my camper."

"Oh. Well that's convenient," Libby said. She pointed to a line on the application. "You do have a cell number, so that's good."

He nodded.

"When can you start?"

"You mean I have the job?"

"It's yours if you want it. Care for a tour of the kitchen?"

"Sure."

The two slid out of the booth, and Marshall followed Libby to the back of the restaurant.

Libby introduced him to Avery and Blake. Libby cocked her head when she realized Avery was giving her the stink eye.

"Can I see you a minute, Libby?" Avery motioned with her chin for Libby to follow.

"Are you kidding me? You hired some dude off the street? A drifter no less? You did see the backpack, didn't you?"

"Shh. He'll hear you." Libby looked over Avery's shoulder and watched as Blake showed him around the kitchen.

"I figured Blake would help me if he got crazy or anything."

Avery knitted her brows tightly. "Please."

"At least go to the local police station and see if he's got a record. Did he even fill out an emergency card?"

"Whoa. Yes, he did." Libby lifted her chin holding out the card.

Avery grabbed it out of her hand. "There's nothing on here. No address, no telephone number, no next of kin. Libby. Come on. What the hell are you doing?"

"I just want to give him a chance," she whispered. "Something about him tells me he needs a friend."

Avery smirked. "What his body language tells me is he is running from something, and it probably is the cops."

"Shh, Avery." Libby whispered.

"I'm going to have Blake check him out. I mean it, Libby. We can't be too careful. This is a weird world we live in." Avery turned and walked toward the two men.

Libby could hear Avery giving Marshall the third degree.

The regulars loved Mrs. Johnson, her smile, and her witty personality. She definitely brought something to the Seaside Café that had been missing before. Hunter learned quickly how to bus the tables, thanks to Mrs. Johnson. They made a great team. Tony was helpful in the kitchen with food prep, and he even tried his hand at cooking some. Marshall was sensitive to Blake's position as head cook, so he took his cues, and appropriately so, from Blake.

Libby secretly visited the police station and inquired about Marshall. They told her they'd follow up with the FBI and let her know if anything materialized.

Libby couldn't put her finger on the reason, but Marshall had a very calming effect on the Seaside Café. She liked having him around. She hoped for everyone's sake he was as innocent as she thought.

It wasn't too long before the café's menu was

updated to include shrimp tacos, shrimp scampi, and mac and cheese with lobster. Marshall was right. They were delicious and a big hit with the customers.

The new crew melded well together, and Libby couldn't have asked for a better team. Luke would have been proud of her selections. The one thing Libby really noticed was that the crew genuinely liked each other. There was no backstabbing, name-calling, or disrespect. Everyone had a job to do and did it well. Libby was bursting at the seams with pride over her newfound friends and coworkers. She felt like they were all getting close.

Day after day, the café produced excellent meals and provided wonderful customer service, and Libby couldn't have been happier. Marshall fit right in with the group, and Mrs. Johnson took the two younger boys under her wing, leaving the business side to Libby and the cooking to Blake.

Libby paced the living room, the business card Jackson had given her mangled in her hand. She plopped down on the sofa and crossed her legs. She uncrossed them, stood, and began pacing the room again. She lowered her eyes to a sleeping Harley.

"What do I say? 'Hi, this is Libby. The one you've been flirting with'."

"How about, 'This is Libby, your new business consultant'."

"Or how about, 'Hey. This is the redhead at the café who's been checking you out'."

"See? I'm no good at this!"

She plopped back down on the cushion staring at her phone. Finally, she picked it up and dialed the number on the business card.

Her heart raced as she anticipated hearing his voice.

"Hello, Jackson Keys here."

"Hi. Jackson. This is Libby." She paused before going on.

"Libby! It's nice to hear your voice. I was hoping you'd call. How are you?"

Libby blew out the breath she'd been holding. This wasn't so strange after all. "I'm doing well. Busy. Um, I'm following up about our discussion."

"Yes. How about dinner?"

"Dinner? Thought you said a working lunch?"

"I know. But you do eat dinner, don't you?" He let out a jovial laugh.

Libby didn't respond. The silence stretched.

"Hello. Are you still there?" He asked.

"Yes. Yes, I'm still here. Dinner sounds lovely," she heard herself saying.

After they made the dinner plans, Libby disconnected the call then phoned the café. Avery answered after the third ring.

"I know you're busy with the dinner shift," Libby said. "I'll be there soon to help close, but I just got off the phone with Jackson and we're going on a dinner date," she said, excitement lacing her words.

"Oh that's great, Libby. Listen, gotta run. Tables are full. See you soon."

After the café closed, Libby and Marshall let everyone go home, and they finished up. Marshall swept and mopped while Libby filled all the salt and pepper shakers and made sure everything was ready on the tables. Tonight, Marshall seemed a bit different. She tried to make small talk with him, but he clammed up. His mysterious side had an allure, and she had to admit, she felt a small attraction toward him, but dismissed it as feelings of friendship and nothing else. After the close call of a kiss, Libby wanted to make sure that Marshall understood that.

The group didn't socialize much beyond the café, mainly because they were always working. But sometimes after the last customer went home, they would turn the sign on the door to "Closed" so they could have dinner together. A bottle of wine would come out, they'd turn on some music and let their hair down to enjoy each other's company. Libby wasn't sure if it was the wine talking, but she got a little wordy with Marshall on one occasion and maybe even stepped over the line a little with her flirting. Wine did that to her.

It was during one of those let-your-hair-down-after-the-café-closed moments that Marshall and Libby had really begun to click. He laughed at her jokes, and she was attentive when he talked about his travels. She listened very intently to all the details, hoping for some hint of what he really was about. She couldn't decide if he was running away from something or in search of something. Maybe a little of both.

Libby felt she and Marshall had actually connected during the latest after-hour party. In fact, he'd almost kissed her. It was during one of these weak, tipsy moments that she'd confided in Marshall about her mixed feelings of keeping the boat. He'd started to lean in for the kiss, but for whatever reason, had hesitated. Libby could feel the awkwardness and had started talking inanely about Mr. Larry, the proprietor of the seafood shop where they bought their local fish.

After the close call of kissing under the influence, Libby had decided it was better to have a strictly platonic relationship with Marshall. Her date with Jackson was coming up. Why would she want to confuse her life with two guys?

LIBBY CHANGED her clothes three times before settling on black slacks and a white cold shoulder flutter blouse.

She sat on the couch waiting for the knock. Her stomach was in knots and eating might not bode well with the queasiness she felt.

The rap on the door made her jump even though he was right on time. She tossed her red locks back and sighed as she crossed over to the door. She opened it wide and smiled.

"Hi," she said.

"Hi, yourself. You look very nice. Are you ready?"

"I am." She grabbed her bag off the counter and stepped outside shutting door behind her.

As they drove down Highway 1, they chatted about things like the weather, mostly the fog, and the café.

"Where shall we go for dinner?" He dropped his gaze from her eyes and focused on her mouth for a moment.

"Oh, wow. You're asking me for recommendations.

Well, let's see. How about the Rip Tide? It's a lovely restaurant overlooking the bay."

"Sounds perfect."

They waited quietly as the hostess prepared their table. Faint sounds could be heard with an occasional spike of laughter. The clanking of utensils and the low tones of people talking as they enjoyed the night out helped ease Libby's nervousness.

The dimly lit restaurant with the white linen table cloths and hot crusty bread with real butter squares seemed to please Jackson. They ordered wine, and as the music played in the background, they got to know each other better. Libby really liked what she found out. Jackson was so much more than just some rich wine mogul.

"So you want to open a wine tasting room here?"

"Yes. What do you think about my idea?"

"I think it's a good one. You're right. We have tons of tourists traveling through here all summer long. It's a great way to showcase your wines. Do you grow red or white grapes?"

Jackson laughed. "You don't know a lot about the wine industry do you?"

Libby shook her head. "Afraid not. I just know I like red wine better."

"I'd be happy to teach you." His eyes swept her before he took a sip of his wine.

She shifted in the chair. "I'd like that."

"I'm happy to see you're a dog lover, too," he said.

Libby smiled. "Harley is the best dog ever."

"Well, I don't know about that. I have a great dog, too," he laughed.

Libby nodded. "I'm sure you do."

"In fact, I'm hosting a huge benefit for the animal shelters in my area. Maybe you'd like to come?

Libby smiled. He wanted to see her again?

"It's next month, so you have plenty of time to rearrange your schedule. Harley is invited, too." Jackson gave a wink.

Libby brought the wine glass up to her lips savoring the sweet aroma before sipping.

"I'll think about it. I probably wouldn't have anything decent enough to wear to such an event."

"It's a summertime event. It's not gowns and tuxes. Well, some will wear that, but it's not necessary. And I'm sure whatever you wear, you'll look beautiful in it. You have the loveliest complexion and your hair…it's stunning."

Libby blushed. Her heart began to beat hard, and she felt as if it would explode. "Thank you. Irish genes."

After dinner, they rode home, talking more about his business plans. He'd found a couple of places, but wasn't sure if they would be good enough. Libby promised to help him scout out some places.

Like a true gentleman he walked her to the door.

"Would you like to come in? Harley loves visitors."

"Sure."

Libby flicked on the kitchen light and moved into the kitchen.

"How about some coffee?" She tossed her bag on the counter.

"Sounds great." He sat on a barstool as she made it.

"I had a great time tonight, Libby."

"Me, too. It was nice to get away from the café. It's my ball and chain." She laughed.

"Time off is very important."

"Well, don't take this wrong, but I'm a working woman and well…you're rich. When I take time off, it's money."

"I know," he softened his voice as he spoke.

Libby sipped her coffee as she eased into this new feeling. Having a man in her house after a date seemed huge. Harley didn't seem to care. Curled up on his bed sound to sleep with no cares in the world all seemed well as far as he was concerned. She pursed her lips and blinked a couple of times.

Jackson twirled around on the stool and looked around the living room. "You have a nice home."

"Thank you. I like it. I wasn't sure if I would in the beginning, but I really do."

Jackson tilted his head. "How so?"

"I'm a city girl. I went to college in San Francisco and we had a condo walking distance to the wharf. When we first moved here, I felt a bit isolated. But after a while, it grew on me, and now, I love it."

"My place is isolated, too," he said.

Libby walked around to where he sat and joined him on the other bar stool. She laced her fingers around the cup and held it on her lap.

"I don't know how to say this except to just say it." She studied his face.

"I've been alone since my husband died. I've thrown all my money, time, and energy into the café, and I'm afraid…"

Jackson leaned in and kissed her. His lips were soft and warm. He gently parted her lips, and when the kiss became more passionate, she drew away.

"Forgive me… I've wanted to do that for some time. I'm sorry if I stepped over the line," he said.

Libby stood up, crossed over to the French doors, and gazed out.

"You're not upset me with are you?" he asked.

"No. I'm just confused."

"About me? About us?"

Libby whirled around. "Us?"

"I thought maybe you felt the same attraction. I have to admit, I didn't know what I would find when I stepped into the Seaside Café that day, but from the first moment I saw you, I felt a pull. Like it was meant to be. Do you believe in things like that?"

Libby crossed over to the stool where he still sat. She placed her cup on the counter. "I do. I believe in those things. I felt it, too. I wasn't sure how to process it, is all." She stepped closer.

He held out his hand and laced his fingers with hers. "Let's just take it slow. See where it goes."

She pulled him up and at the same time leaned in for another kiss. This time, he devoured her mouth with deep sweeping strokes of his tongue.

AFTER ANOTHER LONG day on her feet, Libby headed home with Harley by her side.

The days were getting warmer, something that

didn't happen too often along the coast. Libby loved summertime. Summer was a time for sun, warmth, and tourists. Tourists equaled financial success.

As Libby and Harley trekked back home, every so often, Harley would stop and sniff at a bush, and sometimes he would get the urge to lift his leg. Most of the time he was just marking his territory.

As Libby and Harley rounded the corner to start the short walk up the hill to their house, Libby noticed a familiar shape walking toward them. Bodega was a small town, and most residents knew one another. Strangers were rare. Locals could tell a tourist a mile away. Libby could tell it wasn't a stranger, nor was it a tourist. It was Marshall.

"Hi, Marshall. What are you doing?" Libby asked a bit surprised to see him.

"Taking a walk. Hoping I'd run into you," he said locking his gaze on hers.

"It's a beautiful evening for a walk," she said, ignoring the comment about hoping he'd run into her.

"Yep. It sure is," Marshall responded. "I was hoping to catch you before you left the café. Thought I'd walk you home," he added softly.

"Oh, that's sweet of you, Marshall."

They walked in silence for a few minutes. The only noises between them were the footsteps on the pavement, Harley sniffing, and the rattling of his leash.

"Since you came out here to walk me home, would you like to come in and have a cup of coffee?"

"That would be nice," he said.

Libby unlocked the door and flipped on the lights. She told Marshall to make himself at home, and she went into the kitchen to start the coffee. As the coffee brewed, she made small talk about the busy night at the café. Marshall wasn't very talkative. It was like pulling teeth to get him to converse. Finally, the coffeemaker beeped, signaling that the coffee was made.

"Cream and sugar, right? "Libby asked as she got down two mugs from the cabinet.

"You remembered," he replied.

The two of them sat at the kitchen table, and over coffee, Marshall became an open book, telling Libby how he had left an abusive marriage with only the clothes on his back and his truck. Thank goodness it had a small camper on the back, or he would have been sleeping outside in the elements. He told Libby that as he traveled from Maine, where he and his wife had lived, to the golden coast of California, he had worked odd jobs, mainly in restaurants, earning gas money along the way.

Libby, shocked by the story Marshall told her, was

curious about how his marriage was abusive.

"When you say abusive, what do mean exactly?" Libby peered over her cup as she took a sip.

"She totally abused her own body, and she didn't mind abusing me, too. She'd throw things at me, spit in my face, and at one point even pulled a rifle on me."

Libby's mouth fell open. She heard herself gasp, as Marshall told the story. "Well, I'm glad you feel comfortable enough to talk to me about all of this, Marshall. If there's anything I can do to help you, please don't hesitate to ask."

Libby glanced at her watch. "It's getting late and I think you're opening up with Blake tomorrow, aren't you?"

Marshall took her cue, slid back the chair, and stood.

"Thanks again for listening. And for the coffee, too." He headed toward the front door, pausing just briefly before turning the knob. He turned to face her, his soft brown eyes filled with a little more light than when he'd walked in.

"I'm glad I was able to let you in on some stuff. It will make working at the café easier."

Libby watched as Marshall walked out the door and headed down the walk. She closed the door and locked it. She crossed over to the table and gathered the cups, rinsing them out in the sink. She thought about their conversation. Marshall may have been happy he'd opened up to her, but she wasn't all that convinced he'd told her everything.

LIBBY AND AVERY had the morning off, so she picked up the phone to let Avery in on Marshall's situation.

"I've heard of husbands being abused before, but I've never known any," Avery said.

"I know, right? Can you imagine Blake pulling a gun on you?"

"That would be the last time he ever did that," Avery yelled into the phone. I don't know, Libby. Do you think there is more to the story? You know there's always two sides?"

"I wondered about that. He still remains aloof, and I'm not sure if he's totally come clean with me. I guess he doesn't have to tell me anything more, but we're such a close-knit group. Maybe in time he'll open up more. But for right now, he's sleeping in his camper in the parking lot."

"Maybe you can give him a few more hours so he can move out of the parking lot sooner," Avery said.

"That's a great idea. I don't think the staff would

mind sharing a few hours with him. They seem to like him."

LIBBY KNEW Marshall would be reporting to work soon. She didn't want to be obvious that their last meeting had left her perplexed and confused. She didn't want him to think she was waiting for him either, so she straightened up chairs and gathered the salt and pepper shakers for filling while she waited. She thought about what she would say to him. She hoped he wouldn't see it as charity, but more of a caring gesture. The door opened, setting off the chime. In came Marshall.

"Hello, Marshall," she said as she started to wipe down a table.

He nodded, acknowledging her presence, and then proceeded to walk back to the staff area to clock in. Libby followed him. "Uh, did you sleep well?" Realizing that wasn't the most appropriate thing she could have asked him, she quickly followed it with a request to help her get the tables ready for customers.

"Sure," he replied with a puzzled look on his face. "What's going on? Why do I feel like I just stepped in a pile of dog crap?"

Libby widened her eyes. "What do you mean?" she asked as she straightened up the chairs.

"Is this about what I told you the other night?

Libby stopped, stood straight, and took a deep breath. "I guess. Maybe a little."

"I'm not proud of the fact that I left my wife. But if I'd stayed, someone was going to get hurt. There is only so much mental and physical abuse one can take."

"I know, Marshall. That's not it at all. I'm happy you confided in me, really I am. I just want us to work together smoothly with no more secrets."

"I'm happy for the job. I like having you as a boss," he said narrowing his eyes, keeping them locked onto hers.

Libby unscrewed the lids to the salt and pepper shakers, and Marshall began filling them.

"Libby, I think we need to talk. When I first walked through that door holding the help-wanted card, I saw a friendly face, and for the first time in a very long time, I felt at ease, maybe even at home," he said as he funneled salt into a shaker. "I really needed a friend then, and I think I have one in you," he said as he looked up from pouring salt, staring directly at her.

Libby felt a large lump forming in the hollow of her throat. She swallowed hard and waited for what was to come next.

"You know, I didn't tell you all that stuff about me so you'd feel sorry for me," he said pointedly. "I told you because I needed someone to talk to," he whispered. Libby nodded her head. She still couldn't speak. "I trusted you'd be my confidante … my friend." He reached out and touched her hand.

Libby melted just a little as she stared into his rich brown eyes. She shook off the mesmerized feeling and spoke. "I am your friend, Marshall," she whispered. "I can't help it that I was taken by surprise with your story," she said, lowering her gaze to the table.

He spoke softly, but directly. "What I shared with you last evening cannot change our relationship. You're my employer first, my friend second."

She nodded that she understood.

"Can we put this aside for now?" Marshall asked.

"Of course," Libby said.

Marshall pushed back the chair and rose to his feet. "I'd better go get the chowder started." He crossed the room to the swinging kitchen door and pushed through it leaving Libby standing in the dining room.

OVER THE COURSE of several weeks, Libby tried on numerous occasions to break through Marshall's hard exterior. She knew he had to be hiding something more. Maybe Avery was right. Something was seriously wrong with his situation. She decided to confide in Avery once more. She just needed to air her feelings with the one person who would truly listen and give her honest feedback.

"Let's take a fifteen-minute break and go look for seashells," Libby said to Avery.

Blake gave a head nod that he approved.

Libby told Avery about her frustration with Marshall. Avery was not the least bit sympathetic.

"Just forget about him, will you?" Avery reasoned. "He is playing games. There is something about him I don't like or trust."

"Yeah. You're probably right," Libby said reaching down to pull something shiny out of the wet sand.

"I always thought he was cold and distant," Avery said matter-of-factly.

"I wouldn't say that, Avery. He's definitely not a real open kind of guy, but he did share a lot with me. I just think there might be more we don't know." She paused, then added, "But do we really need to know? I think I'm wasting too much time wondering what his real deal is, ya know?"

"Girl, I couldn't have said it any better. I wanted to tell you a long time ago to fire him."

"Fire him! That's a bit much, don't you think?"

Avery dug her foot into the sand then looked off into the distance. "Yeah, I guess so. Let's talk about someone more interesting…what about Jackson?"

Libby squared her shoulders, and pulled her brows together as she looked straight into her friend's eyes.

"What?" Avery said laughing at Libby.

"I'm surprised at you, Avery. You're a married woman."

"I may be married, but I'm not dead. That man is gorgeous."

"I don't get to see much of him except when he occasionally comes in to have lunch.

"Is your hand broken? Have you forgotten how to use a phone…I mean I know you're a bit technologically challenged, but…" Avery smiled.

"I know. I need to. It's just so new for me. But, If it's something I want, I've learned I can't be afraid of the challenge." Libby smiled back.

"I hope my hints weren't too subtle about being interested. I was afraid to come on too strong with what happened between Marshall and me."

Libby looked out across the bay.

"I just felt that maybe he was hoping for more from me."

"Like a relationship?" Avery asked.

"Uh-huh," Libby whispered.

"No way! You and the drifter?" Avery laughed.

"What's so funny. He's good looking in a mysterious man sort of way," Libby said grasping for words.

"Whatever. You're much better off with Jackson and his gorgeous dimples, lean body, strong hands…"Avery smiled.

"I see you've noticed," Libby said knocking shoulders with her.

"Who hasn't!"

Libby felt better once she'd talked to Avery. She was too old for games and drama. She decided to put Marshall out of her mind the best she could. He was an excellent worker, and she didn't want to change their working relationship. She'd just be careful to not be left alone with him to avoid any more unnecessary conversations.

Libby worked less hours now that she had a full team. It felt good to be able to sleep in a little and go home a earlier. It gave her more time to sketch and paint, something she really enjoyed doing and was good at.

After a morning of sketching boats in the bay, Libby headed to the café.

Concentrating on refilling the soda machines, she heard the familiar sound of the wind chime. She looked up, and standing there in the doorway was Jackson. "Good afternoon," Libby blurted out.

"Good afternoon to you," Jackson responded.

"Your regular table awaits," Libby said as she led Jackson to his favorite spot.

Jackson sat. Libby started to ask him if he wanted his usual—clam chowder with all the toppings, but Jackson instead said, "Please sit down for a minute?"

Libby, startled by the request, obliged him. She signaled for Mrs. Johnson. "Could you get us a cup of coffee?" Libby said.

Libby couldn't help but admire Jackson's cute dimples. Even with his salt and pepper hair, Jackson was handsome. Still, a cold tremor ran through her body. "What's going on?" she muttered under her breath.

Jackson's body tensed. "I'd like to know if you'll be my guest this weekend," he said.

Libby's body went rigid with hearing the words. She cocked her head a little to the side, furrowing her brow.

The nonverbal language made Jackson laugh out loud. "I'd like you to come up to my winery in Sonoma.

You never gave me an answer about the fundraiser for the local animal shelters. There'll be lots of food, wine, and entertainment. As I said, you can bring Harley, too," he added, smiling. "It would make me happy if you'd say 'yes'."

"Thank you for the invitation. It does sound fun, but I'd like a few more days to think about it." She really needed to figure out the logistics. Spending the weekend with him was a big leap. "Can I let you know Thursday?"

"Certainly," he said as he flashed a grin.

Her eyes went straight to his dimples. She felt her face flush. "Okay. Well, back to work," she said.

She walked into the kitchen to find Blake and Marshall talking. They stopped when she walked in. Libby sensed that they may have been talking about her. Libby wasn't quite sure how to handle the awkward situation. She suddenly felt like a stranger in her own café.

Avery had the day off, so except for Mrs. Johnson, Libby didn't have any girl power to help her.

She took off her apron. "I'm going out for a bit. You guys handle the lunch crowd," she said throwing her apron on a chair and then exiting through the back door.

CHAPTER SIX

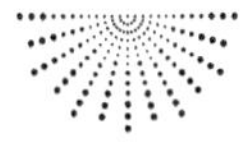

Libby put the leash on Harley, and the two of them went for a walk down to the pier. She was hoping that just maybe Sam and the *Salty Dog* would be at the dock. She really needed to see him. He'd be the voice of reason for her.

Just as she'd hoped, Sam was at the dock. The boat and her crew were in for the day, and Sam had just finished cleaning her. Now she'd be ready for the next run. Sam looked up and saw Libby and Harley. He waved.

"Hey, Libby," he said as she approached the boat.

"Hi," she said quickly. "Can I come aboard?"

"Sure," he said hesitantly.

Libby wasn't exactly sure how to start the conversation with Sam. She had to remember that Sam was Luke's best friend first and hers second. She started talking about how long it had been since Luke had passed away. Then she threw into the mix quickly about men coming into her life, and at odd times and under strange circumstances.

"Whoa, wait a minute"

Libby folded her arms. "I know I'm behaving like some school girl with a crush. I don't know what I really expect you to say."

"If you're asking me if Luke would mind that you want to start dating, I can answer that," Sam said matter-of-factly.

Libby nodded.

"Is that what you want to know?" he asked her again. Sam assured her that she had grieved long enough. "You'll always love Luke. Dating and moving on with your life, Libby, is not in any way showing disrespect for him. He would want you to go on living."

Libby gave Sam a big hug.

He chuckled and hugged her back. "Okay, now that we got that settled, who's going to be the lucky guy?" Sam asked Libby.

Libby felt her cheeks warm. She hesitated, and then she told Sam all about Jackson.

When the conversation slowed, she added, "By the way, I wanted to talk to you about a business proposition."

Sam cocked his head. "Another business proposition?"

"Well. It's still about the boat. I want to sell it to you."

Sam's rubbed his jaw. "I don't have the funds to buy it, Libby. We've been over that before."

"Just hear me out. I'm willing to work something out. Maybe I could sell you half the boat?" She smiled.

"Be co-owners?"

Libby nodded.

"Maybe," he said slowly.

"Eventually you could buy me out. I really don't want to own it much longer. This was Luke's dream, and I supported him in it when he was alive. But I have my own dreams to pursue," Libby said.

Libby took a few steps back. "Just think about it. I have to run. I'll be in touch." She and Harley picked up their pace, and as they made their way off the boat, Libby looked back once toward Sam and smiled.

As Libby and Harley neared the café, she thought about Jackson's date proposal. She loved animals, wine, music, and good food. It sounded like a splendid way to spend a weekend. She'd let him know tomorrow when he stopped in for lunch. Now that the café had extra staff, going away for a short weekend should not present any issues. She couldn't wait to let Avery know.

Libby had a hard time getting to sleep that night. She tossed and turned for several hours, only to finally give in to exhaustion.

The next morning, Harley lazily watched Libby with one eye open as she got up and turned on lights. He softly moaned as she petted him. "Let's get an early start down at the café, Harley."

By the time Avery and Blake showed up for work, Libby had all the tables set up and the coffee and tea made, as well as the pitchers of refreshing cucumber ice water. Libby also had peeled potatoes and chopped onions for the clam chowder.

"Wow, did you spend the night here last night?" Blake asked.

Libby turned around with a big smile on her face.

Avery looked her over and smiled back. "No, I think it's a case of butterflies," Avery said as she lovingly jabbed Blake's side with her elbow.

Blake returned the jab with a hard stare.

Libby hummed and sang as she rinsed and stacked dishes in the dishwasher.

"Can I see you a minute?" Avery asked.

Libby followed Avery to the dining room.

"You must have reported to work at the crack of dawn to get this much accomplished."

Libby hummed while she worked.

"Do you have some big, juicy secret that you want to share. There's only so much humming and singing I can tolerate." Avery said.

Libby turned her back on Avery and began to wipe down the menus. "Can't a person come to work early? I mean really, what crime is that?"

"Okay, I can see that I'm not going to get anywhere with you." Avery started to walk away.

Libby gently grabbed her wrist. "Oh, what's the use? You can see right through me anyway," Libby said, lowering her head. "It's just that Jackson asked me to go up to his estate for the weekend," Libby said, raising her head back up and looking for any disapproval from her friend.

"That's fantastic, Libby. I really like Jackson. He seems like such a nice fellow. You did tell him yes, didn't you?" Avery asked.

"I told him I needed time to think about it," Libby replied.

"Girl, you'd better get your act together and go on that weekend getaway," Avery stated.

Libby smiled. "Are you sure?"

"Yes, it's absolutely all right to go away for the weekend. That's why we hired the additional personnel. We'll be okay. You go and have a great time. We can take care of Harley for you, too."

"No need. Harley is coming with me. The benefit is for the local animal shelter."

"How cool," Avery said. She hesitated a second, then added, "Not to change the subject, but Blake and I could use a few days off, too. Maybe when you get back?"

Libby's hand flew to her mouth. "Oh, Avery. How unthoughtful of me. You and Blake have been busting your butts for me, and I've been so preoccupied with Jackson…and Marshall, that I forgot to think of my two best employees."

"It's okay. Blake and I just started thinking about it. We're good. We'll discuss it when you get back." Avery hugged Libby.

Just like clockwork, Jackson showed up for lunch.

Libby sat down at the table with him. "I've thought about it long and hard. I want you to know I did not make this decision lightly. I even talked it over with my best friend, Avery. I would love to accept your invitation."

Jackson reached across the table and gently put his

hand on hers. "I think you'll have a wonderful time. Thank you for accepting. Sometimes it's good to do something you'd not normally do." His words were slow and deliberate, and Libby's heart jumped at his hopeful look.

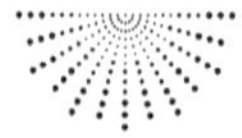

LIBBY PACKED a small overnight bag for her trip to Jackson's estate. She wasn't exactly sure what to take, but she knew she would need at least something appropriate for the event night and then casual wear for the rest of the weekend. No one actually dressed up in California it seemed, so as she looked through her closet to fill her bag, she kept that in mind. In the end, she packed linen capris, a sleeveless baby blue button-down blouse, a pair of brown leather sandals, a black-and-white summer print dress, and white sandals, and then she threw in a pair of gray walking shorts and a white polo-style shirt. She decided on a lightweight gown and robe and her slippers for bedtime. She didn't wear much makeup, so she tossed her ever-essential moisturizer, mascara, and blush, along with her hair-brush and toothbrush, into her toiletry bag, and she was all set.

Jackson had told Libby he would pick her up around noon. The big gala event didn't start until seven. He wanted her to have a chance to get unpacked and have a look around before the crowd gathered. It was getting close to the time he'd be arriving. She glanced around to see if she had forgotten anything. She suddenly realized she needed to gather Harley's dog food and bed. She went out to the kitchen to get those things ready when there was a knock at the door.

"Hi, Libby, I know I'm a bit early," Jackson said as he entered the house.

"Oh, that's okay. I'm just getting Harley's food together, and then we'll both be ready," she said as she walked into the kitchen. Libby felt awkward, as if Jackson was watching her intently. She went to the cupboard, got out Harley's food, and scooped several cups into a large Ziploc baggie. She walked down the hallway into the bedroom to get his bed. She called out, "I'll be right back."

When she returned with Harley's bed, Jackson was standing where she'd left him, and he was holding the dog food in one hand and, in the other, Harley's leash.

Harley sat next to him, tail wagging, ready to go, and Libby's heart melted a little. "I hope you don't mind. I went ahead and leashed him up," Jackson said with a big smile.

"No worries," Libby replied. "Thanks for doing that." The three of them left the house, and as Libby locked the front door, Jackson put Harley in the back-seat of his four-door Ford truck.

The silence in the truck was very odd. Libby wasn't sure what to say, and Jackson wasn't offering up anything either. Finally, after several minutes of awkward silence, Libby broke it by asking Jackson how long a ride it was to his estate. That little question opened up the floodgates to the conversation, and before Libby realized it, they were pulling into the long driveway of the Jackson Keys Estate Winery.

Local native vegetation lined the entrance to the winery. There was an occasional boulder strategically placed here and there to add to the beautiful rustic charm of the estate. Flowering trees and shrubs added to the beauty of the property, and as they drove farther, Libby got a glimpse of the estate itself, and her jaw dropped. She let out a gasp and then looked at Jackson.

"This is your place?" she said.

"Yes. This property has been in my family for over

fifty years. Welcome to the Jackson Keys Estate Winery," he declared.

Jackson turned the truck into a circular driveway that took them to the front of a beautiful ranch-style home. Libby couldn't take her eyes off the grand home. Jackson came around to the passenger side of the truck and opened the door. He reached his hand out to her. "Come on, I can't wait for you to meet my staff."

Libby took his hand and stepped down. The feel of her hand in his caused a stirring deep in the pit of her stomach. Her eyes darted from the grand front door to the landscaped yards and back to the front of the house.

Jackson jogged to the other side of the truck to let out Harley and retrieve her bags. He quickly pulled her bags out and rejoined her.

He fixed his eyes on her face. "Okay, are we ready?" he said, his voice softening a little.

Libby widened her smile.

Jackson clasped her hand in his and they made their way toward the beautiful ornate double doors.

Holding Harley's leash, Libby gingerly stepped inside. She expected that his home would be grand, but she had no idea just how special his place would be. Her gaze moved from a beautiful console table with a very large vase full of flowers to a massive fireplace she could see in the distance. She felt like a kid in a candy store.

"Your home is beautiful, Jackson," she said as she stopped to admire a painting.

"My grandmother painted that," Jackson said with pride.

"It's beautiful," she enthused.

"She just did it as a hobby," he added.

"I dabble in watercolors," she said softly.

"You must share your work. I'd love to see them," he said, taking her arm.

They made their way to the large living room. She'd already seen the fireplace from the foyer. It was the focal point for the room. She walked up to the over-sized mantel and stared at each photograph.

Motioning for her to sit, Jackson plopped down on the oversized leather sofa. Libby followed suit taking a seat next to him while Harley lay down on the corner of a colorful area rug.

She turned her body slightly so she could focus on his face.

"Your house is absolutely beautiful."

He let out a small laugh. "I think you already said that." He gently touched her knee. Her eyes went straight to his hand. He quickly removed it, placing it on the seat cushion between them.

Libby's eyes focused on a figure she saw coming from another area of the house. A nice looking man, probably in his late fifties, flashed a wide grin as he approached them.

"Good evening, sir."

"Good evening, Carl. This is Libby. She'll be our guest this weekend. And this," he said pointing to the reposing dog, is Harley."

Carl stood in a very stoic stance, shifting his nod from Libby to Harley.

She flashed a smile and gave a quick wave. "Nice to meet you, Carl."

"Can you please take her bags to her room?"

"Absolutely, sir. My pleasure."

"We're going to take a walk outside and see how things are coming along," Jackson said and stood.

Libby followed his lead and joined him.

"Very well, sir. Let me know if you need anything."

Jackson grabbed Libby's hand and they set off for the grand tour.

"Oh, my word, Jackson. This is like a beautiful oasis back here. It's like I'm on an island."

Jackson laughed.

Libby smiled when she saw the large swimming pool, cabanas, wood trellises, and several sitting areas which made up Jackson's *backyard*. "I just can't believe you live like this.

"I wasn't born with a silver spoon in my mouth. My family has worked this land for generations. I'm very proud of what my ancestors accomplished so that our legacy continues."

"You should be. It is just—"

"Beautiful?" he asked, cutting her off.

She teasingly smacked him on the shoulder. "I'm sorry I can't find any other adjectives to describe your place."

"I'm blessed, that's for sure." He said, grinning.

He put his arm around her waist and pulled her close. Their faces were just inches apart. She swallowed hard. It felt like she had a golf ball in her throat. She dropped Harley's leash. Jackson started to lean in for a kiss when another employee suddenly appeared, offering them a drink. Libby stepped back and covered her mouth with her hand. Jackson cleared his throat.

"Thank you," he said taking two wine glasses off a silver tray.

"This is one of our chardonnays." He lifted his glass. "To a great weekend," he toasted as they clinked their glasses.

They finished their wine as they meandered the pathways and enjoyed the beautiful landscape around them. "You probably would like to see your room and get settled before the party. I have some loose ends to take care of as well. The kennel staff can take Harley and let him meet my dogs as they await the other four-legged guests while you check out your accommodations for the weekend. Let me show you the way to your room, madam," Jackson said.

Libby immediately saw the great big smile and the twinkle in his eyes that she'd become fond of. Yes, this would be a great weekend indeed.

After Jackson left her at her room, Libby couldn't believe the accommodations at the estate. Her room was large and decorated with fine art and fabrics. On the walls were beautiful oil paintings depicting vineyards and other landscapes unique to California. The furniture was beautiful, rich mahogany wood and the bed was decked out with a white comforter and several embroidered pillows with California native flowers on them. She brushed her hand across the colorful thread. Orange for poppies, purple for cornflowers, and red for geraniums.

In one corner of the room sat a beautiful uphol-stered chair. In another corner, a large armoire housed a television. Along one of the walls sat a large marble-topped vanity with a white leather-covered stool under-neath. On the top of the vanity sat a lighted mirror and several bottles of expensive perfume. She picked up one of the bottles and sprayed a little on her wrist. She took a whiff of the light floral fragrance.

Libby couldn't help herself. She ran her hand over all the furniture. She sat on the bed and bounced on it. She jumped off the bed and rushed over to the French doors to see outside. She looked out and was amazed by the view. She had her own veranda, complete with a table, chairs, and a small bar. She walked back inside. A place this fancy would have to have a great bathroom, too!

The bathroom was the size of her bedroom back in Bodega. There was a large whirlpool tub and a huge separate shower that had multiple spray nozzles, including one huge rain shower overhead. She really was beginning to feel pampered. The walls were a warm gold color, and the floor was tiled in white marble just like the foyer. The towels were yellow with the same embroidered flowers she had seen on the pillows. Impressive oil paintings and some watercolors ornamented the bathroom as well. She wondered if Jackson's grandmother had painted them.

Libby unpacked her suitcase and decided she would freshen up. She wanted to try out that fancy shower. After showering, Libby wrapped herself in a luxurious robe she found hanging on a hook behind the door. In a cubby behind the door, she found matching slippers. She felt as if she was at a famous spa getting the full treatment.

She already knew what she would be wearing to the event, so she laid everything out and began to blow-dry her hair when her phone rang.

CHAPTER EIGHT

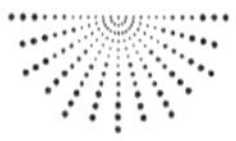

"Hey, there," Avery said. "I hope I didn't disturb you. I just thought I should fill you in on your other admirer," she stated in a quirky tone.

"Oh? What do you mean?" Libby asked.

"Marshall. He's been asking about you. I just told him you'd be back in a few days. He gives me the creeps, Libby."

"Now, Avery. Don't exaggerate. He's fine."

"I think he likes you more than you think."

"Well, I'll straighten it out when I get back."

Avery laughingly said, "Since I have you on the phone, how are the accommodations at the winery?"

"Oh, Avery, you'd not believe it unless you saw pictures. Trust me, I am taking a lot of them, so you can see. This suite is like none I have ever stayed in. I better go and finish getting ready for the big event, though. See you tomorrow sometime. Give everyone my love." Libby crossed over to the large window and peeked out.

Libby finished getting ready. She slipped on the black-and-white print dress that fell to her ankles. The dress had a slit up one side and was made out of a lightweight polyester and cotton blend fabric. She admired herself in the long mirror on the door. She sat down on the bench and strapped on her sandals. She finished up by applying her makeup and brushing her hair. White gold hoop earrings and a white gold bracelet completed her look. Libby spritzed on some of the fancy perfume and decided she was ready for whatever the night would bring.

There was a light tap on her door. Libby opened it to find Jackson standing there. He looked very handsome. He was dressed in a pair of dark khaki slacks and a blue chambray button-down shirt—and he smelled good, too.

"Perfect timing," Libby said. "I just finished getting ready. You look very nice," she added." Her cheeks flushed when he winked at her.

"You take my breath away." She watched mesmerized as he lifted her hand to his lips. "The guests should be arriving shortly," Jackson said. "I have the kennel staff getting Harley all ready for his debut. They gave him and the other dogs a bath and brushed their coats."

"Thank you," Libby replied.

The two of them took a detour to the kitchen. Jackson told Libby he wanted to check on the cooks and the food preparation. When they entered the kitchen, Libby could not believe the size of it. It was several sizes larger than the one at the café.

Libby looked around. It had two stoves, an enormous stainless steel refrigerator, and counter space she'd never seen before in a kitchen. However, she'd never seen a kitchen this large before, either. Jackson spoke to the chefs and got an idea of how things were progressing. He was smiling and nodding, so Libby felt all was good. The food looked good and smelled even better. She couldn't wait to try some. She remembered she'd not really eaten a lot and was getting hungry.

Jackson signaled for Libby to follow him. They moved through the kitchen, and after weaving their way through various hallways and doors, they exited onto the outdoor patio. The overhead trellises were decorated with twinkling white lights, and the music was playing softly through cleverly placed speakers. Looking around, Libby saw tables set up, draped with white linen cloths and candles placed in the center of each, all surrounding the sparkling swimming pool. Libby and Jackson continued to make the rounds of the area. People had not arrived yet; Jackson was just making sure things were set.

In one corner stood what would be one of the most visited areas—the bar, with the bartender already at his post. Just quickly looking, Libby saw top-shelf vodka and whiskey and, of course, bottles of wine. Continuing on, they both made their way to the various food tables. Chafing dishes were lined up one after another. Jackson lifted the tops and peered in. The first one had saffron rice, chicken, chorizo sausage, and jumbo shrimp. The rice was a beautiful golden yellow with the saffron. The paella would surely be a big hit. The next one Jackson looked into had shredded pork.

"Let's go over to the cold foods and check them out," Jackson said.

Several salads, relishes, cooked shrimp on ice, and even sushi rolls of several varieties were lined up. There was something available to stimulate everyone's taste buds. Libby's mouth was watering. She again remembered she hadn't eaten much and thought she should have something before she started drinking any alcohol. She made a mental note that as soon as it was appropriate, she would head to the appetizer table where crackers, dips, cheese, and other bite-size delicacies awaited.

Libby knew at some point the dogs were going to enter. After all, this was an event to benefit the local animal shelters. "When do the dogs come out and meet the guests?" Libby asked.

"After dinner," Jackson replied, as he stepped a bit closer to her. Libby wasn't sure what the significance of this movement was, but it made her heart beat a lot faster, and her palms became sweaty. She was hoping he would kiss her.

"We're going to have a bit of a social hour and a silent auction. Then we'll eat, and finally the dogs will have their moment. How does that sound?" Jackson said as he took Libby's hands in his.

"That sounds great," she responded, feeling a bit strange with him holding her hands. It had been a long time since she had been intimate with anyone except Luke. But she had to admit that it felt good —felt right.

Guests started to arrive, and soon the entire back-yard was full of local businessmen and their wives, as well as Jackson's friends and extended family. Just as Libby promised herself, she made her way to the appe-tizer table. With a glass of chardonnay in one hand and a plate of cheese cubes, raw vegetables, dip, and crackers in the other, she filled up her stomach so the wine wouldn't go to her head.

Jackson introduced her to many people that night. He told each one of them about the Seaside Café in Bodega. He recommended everyone visit. She did a lot of blushing that evening. Jackson didn't even know about the *Salty Dog*. She'd never really had the opportunity to tell him. She made another mental note to share that information with him at some point. Everyone Libby met was so kind. It turned out they were all animal lovers and many had several animals in their households, too. Libby concluded that people who have animals, and love them as much as she did, had very kind hearts. It was going to be a great evening.

The music stopped, and Jackson made an announcement. "May I please have your attention? Please, everyone, settle down for just a minute." The group looked his way. "We are all here tonight to raise money for a very worthy cause. The local animal shelters need many supplies to keep the animals healthy and happy while they await their forever homes. I appreciate you all coming to support the event, and I hope you are having a great time.

"We are going to start the silent auction now. Behind me, along the back hedges, we have tables lined up with various items," Jackson said with sweeping arms. "Please be generous. All of the proceeds will go to the shelters. We will give it about thirty minutes, and then we'll eat. After dinner, we will announce the winners. Have fun bidding. Thank you all very much."

Jackson raised his glass. The entire group erupted in, "Cheers!" and then they all scattered at the auction tables.

Libby walked toward the tables that displayed the auction items. She saw wine glasses etched with initials, wine glasses with colorful stems, and ceramic spoon rests and trivets decorated with grapes and wine bottles. Olive oil and a variety of balsamic vinegars were also available for auction. Libby reached down and picked up a large white envelope with a big, fancy C on the front. She opened it up. Inside was a gold embossed card she recognized as a gift certificate to a very famous spa for a day of pampering.

Libby continued weaving her way down and around the various tables to see the great items. All of a sudden, she felt a tap on her shoulder. She twirled around to come face-to-face with Jackson. "Do you see anything you just have to have?" he asked with a smile.

"The gift certificate to the spa would be nice," she remarked, looking straight into his dark blue eyes.

They both continued looking at items, greeting

those who made eye contact, and just enjoying the evening.

"It's just about time. If you want to bid on something, do it now. I'm going to be ringing the bell in about five minutes," Jackson said as he brushed past her to greet a local businessman.

Libby thought about what he'd said. She walked back to where the gift certificate was and looked at the clipboard beside it. There were ten bids for the item, ranging from fifty to five hundred dollars. She realized this was out of her league. She glanced around the room. It was full of women and men dressed in their best, and she'd never seen so many diamonds at one place. She wondered what they were thinking about her in her chain store outfit and knock off designer jewelry. She took a sip of her wine and went to find her table.

As Jackson promised, he rang the bell, letting everyone know the auction was over. The guests started making their way to the tables for dinner. After everyone had found his or her seat, Jackson rang the bell once more.

"Thank you, everyone, for finding your seats quickly. We have a lovely dinner waiting for us. We are going to start by table. Please help yourself to the delicious food that has been lovingly prepared by my own chef and his staff. Thank you again for joining me this evening. Table five, please help yourself to the food." Libby and Jackson were sitting at table eight. She wasn't starving since she had nibbled on the great appetizers. She and Jackson would wait their turn.

Dinner was fantastic, just as she knew it would be. The chef and his staff had really outdone themselves. Libby couldn't remember a time when she'd enjoyed her dinner this much. Well, maybe the time she and Luke had dined at their favorite restaurant in San Francisco.

Jackson rang the bell for the last time, announcing it was time to reveal the winners of the silent auction. He had one of his assistants read off the names. One by one, people came up to claim their items. Libby wasn't sure at first if it really was her own name being called. She knew she had not bid on anything, so it must be another Libby. After his assistant had called out the name twice, Jackson grabbed the microphone, looked right at her, and said, "Libby, that's you."

With a surprised look on her face, she proceeded to the podium. The wine had made her a bit tipsy, so she didn't even remember going up. Jackson handed her a white envelope. She looked at it and instantly recognized the big fancy C from earlier.

"I didn't bid on this," she mumbled to him.

"A secret admirer did," Jackson said as he winked at her.

Libby could feel her face becoming hot. She touched her head and wiped the moisture from her forehead. Here heart fluttered and her stomach gathered and pulled as she held the envelope in her hand. This one gesture from Jackson said more than he might know.

Libby made her way back to the table. She felt like everyone was staring at her. *It must be the wine making me paranoid*, she thought. Jackson made his way over to her after all the winners collected their prizes.

"I hope you don't mind, but I got it for you. I know how you were admiring it. It's for a great cause, after all," he added, sensing he may have overstepped by giving her such a lavish gift.

Libby didn't know what to say. She finally muttered, "Thank you."

Libby felt something on her leg, so she took her hand and brushed at it. She felt a cold nose. She looked down, and there was Harley, wagging his tail. She reached down and hugged him and then looked up to see the grounds covered with four-legged friends. Playing in the background was the song, "Who Let the Dogs Out?" Libby pushed her chair back and stood up. She briefly looked around the pool area. "Let's go mingle," she whispered. Libby made her way through the crowd, Harley following one paw step behind.

After all the guests had left, Libby and Jackson were alone in the living room.

"I think tonight was a great hit. Between the silent auction and donations for dinner, we collected over ten thousand dollars. We'll have to calculate it more accurately in the coming days."

"That's a lot of money. It will definitely purchase a lot of items for the shelters." Libby widened her grin, her eyes sparkled with joy.

"It's been a lovely evening, Jackson," Libby said as she gathered her spa certificate and her evening bag. "Thanks again for inviting me—and Harley, too," she added quickly, admiring Harley's shiny coat.

As the two of them walked through the interior of his sprawling home holding hands, Libby's mind filled with thoughts of what a great evening they'd had. Great food, wonderful-tasting wines, interesting company, and the big surprise of the night—the silent auction.

"Here we are," Jackson said as he gestured toward her bedroom door.

Libby's eyes widened. "Sorry. I didn't realize. I admit I get a little lost in your house. It's like a hotel," she said as she backed up against the door.

He held her hand in his, and as he traced her fingers, he gently swayed their hands in a soft back and forth motion. "I'm so happy you accepted my invitation tonight," he whispered.

Libby felt her face soften at his words. He stepped closer bringing her hand up to his lips. "You're so beautiful."

She felt a smile soften her features, and then his lips were on hers. He slid his hand behind her head running his fingers through her hair and down her back. It sent shivers up her spine. They deepened the kiss, their tongues dancing to a heated tango. He reached around and turned the bedroom door knob opening the door. The abruptness of the door opening threw them both off-balance. They recovered quickly, and he walked her backwards into the room. Shutting the door with a quick kick from his foot, Jackson led her to the big bed. She lay back across it looking at him hungrily and let out a breath slowly as he joined her.

Libby woke to the sun shining in her eyes. She'd forgotten to close the blinds all the way. She stretched her arms out wide, yawned, and then realized she had a little headache from the overdose of fun the night before. Her mouth felt parched, and when she touched her mouth she remembered the night with Jackson, too.

She needed coffee. She got out of bed and jumped in the shower. She let the hot water hit her in the face for several minutes. It didn't take the place of coffee, but it would help. She dressed, packed her bag, and took one more look around the gorgeous room.

The house was soundless. Eerily quiet. Libby and Harley made their way down the various hallways. The aroma of freshly ground coffee beans led her to the kitchen. Once inside, she saw that the kitchen was empty. She looked around and spotted the coffeemaker. She decided the cups must be nearby. She opened a cabinet, and luckily, the first one she opened contained the mugs. She reached up to get one when a man's voice startled her.

"I see you found the coffee," Jackson said.

Libby slowly turned. "Yes. The aroma of it led me straight here," she said, giggling. As Libby poured herself a cup of the dark roast, she realized she was rude not to offer Jackson a cup. "Would you care to join me?" Libby suggested.

"Yes. That would be nice." Jackson pulled two chairs out from the table for them.

Libby carried the two cups of steaming hot java to the table. She sat down and started to play with her mug a bit before taking her first sip. That first sip of coffee was like a miracle drug. She let out a big sigh. "Wow. This coffee is delicious," she said matter-of-factly.

Jackson replied, "Yup."

Jackson cleared his throat. "About last night …"

Libby waited.

"I hope what happened isn't going to make this all weird."

"Not at all," Libby said, telling a little lie. The fact of the matter was, she felt a little strange now that they'd crossed that bridge. She wasn't sure why, because quite frankly she'd wanted it as badly as he had.

"Are you having regrets? Because I'm not," she said, circling the top of her cup with her finger.

"No," he said, taking her hand. "It's wish you could stay a little longer …"

She quickly looked up from her cup. "I have a business to run. You, better than anyone, should understand why I have to get back to the café."

He nodded. "Yes, but it'll be there tomorrow. I want this to be our time—our little getaway from all the daily throes of business."

"We'll do it again. I had a great time. This overnight was just what I needed to recharge," she said, smiling.

"Very well." He scooted his chair back from the table and stood up. Libby lifted her chin so she could still make eye contact with him. He towered over her.

"I'll be waiting outside when you're ready, but I have a few things to take care of first."

Libby watched as he left. She tilted her head and pursed her lips. "*Relationships. The struggle can be real.*" she mused. She picked up her cup and took a sip of the now cold brew. She quickly took inventory of the kitchen to find the microwave.

CHAPTER NINE

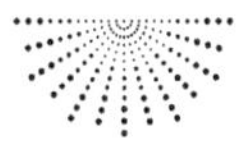

Libby and Harley walked up the driveway leading to their front door. She turned and waved at Jackson. She watched as he drove off. She sighed. Feelings for him were beginning to form. She hoped they could make this work. Long distance relationships could be difficult.

Once inside, Libby put her bags in the bedroom and then sat down on the couch. Harley plopped out on the floor near her feet. The house was quiet—too quiet. Libby got up and opened the French doors so she could hear the sounds of the tide as it hit the beach, and other pleasant sounds unique to the bay she loved so.

Deciding to delay going in to work, she checked in with the café instead, promising to come in soon, and looked over the mail. She took out her painting supplies and headed to the seashore park. She needed a little more time to settle after what had happened last night, and the fresh air would do her good.

She opened up her folding chair and easel and looked around for some inspiration. She found it quickly. A patch of colorful flowers gently blowing in the breeze and an old man walking a small dog. She smiled as she sketched. Every now and then, thoughts of the passionate night with Jackson entered her mind. She knew Avery would want details. How much she would share still remained to be seen, or heard.

After a few hours of watching people and pets, Libby headed home. She'd put off going to the café long enough.

Libby walked into the café, feeling as if she'd been gone longer than overnight. A few of the tables had patrons seated at them.

She nodded toward the old guy who came in every day and gave a quick wave to the giggling girls waiting for Hunter. She'd get caught up with Avery after she finished helping a customer. Libby walked back to the kitchen. She had never been so happy to smell the clam chowder simmering on the stove. Everything felt so much more vivid and new today.

"Hey, look who's back!" Blake shouted.

Avery ran up to Libby and hugged her. Blake shot Libby an enormous grin with the promise of a hug later when he wasn't so busy.

"Where's the rest of the staff?" Libby asked as she peered inside the simmering pot.

"Mrs. Johnson reports at ten thirty, and Tony comes in around eleven thirty. I have Hunter on the schedule for one thirty.

"Well Hunter's little gals are out there waiting for him now. Someone should let them know he's not scheduled until later."

Avery laughed. "Marshall has the day off," she added, glancing at Libby as she stirred the clam chowder.

Libby nodded. "Sounds like you've got everything under control," Libby said quickly.

"Did you expect anything less?" Avery asked.

Libby smiled. "Not really."

The lunch rush was soon over, and Libby and Avery found themselves seated at a corner table drinking a refreshing glass of homemade iced tea. Libby ran her hand up and down the glass, wiping the condensation on a nearby napkin.

"Well, I'm waiting," Avery said impatiently.

Libby looked up from playing with her glass. "What?" she snapped back.

"Oh, come on, Libby. Details. I need details, please," Avery retorted.

Libby cleared her throat. "It was very lovely," she whispered.

"It was lovely," Avery repeated. "You can't give me anything else besides 'lovely'?"

"The food was excellent, the music was fantastic, and the accommodations were out of this world," Libby told Avery. She slid her phone over to Avery so she could look at the pictures she'd taken.

"So, you had a great time," Avery said as she scrolled through the images. "What about Jackson?" she asked.

"He was a gentleman. He has many friends. A lot of money was raised for the animal shelters. It was a very nice event," Libby said.

"I'm glad you had a terrific time. What about chemistry?" Avery asked Libby as she peered deep into her eyes for an answer.

Libby fidgeted a bit in her seat before answering. "The chemistry is out of the world." Libby felt like some school girl talking about her Friday night kiss. She wasn't sure she really wanted to tell her everything. She wanted to savor it for herself for a bit.

Taking the hint, Avery said, "The café has been quite busy this weekend. I haven't figured up the sales, but I think it's safe to say it will exceed expectations," Avery said cheerfully. "Marshall has been so helpful, as has the entire staff. We should plan a little barbecue to celebrate our excellent team," she added.

Libby agreed. "Let's look at the calendar and make that happen."

Just then, the wind chime jingled. Libby looked up to see Marshall coming in. Marshall walked over to them.

"Don't want to interrupt you ladies, just wanted to say welcome home, Libby."

"Thanks. It's nice to be home."

"So things are going better with Marshall?" Libby whispered to Avery.

"Yeah. He does what he's supposed to. I still think something is off with him. I just don't know what it is."

Libby frowned. "You're never going to let that go, are you?"

"Just call me Agent Avery." She laughed.

"The police report was clean, so Agent Avery won't find anything either." Libby pushed back her chair and stood. "I don't feel like working today."

"That's love talking right there," Avery smiled.

"Love after one night?"

"Night? Did you guys spend the night together?" Avery's eyes widened.

Libby touched her shoulder. "Some details must not be disclosed. Not even to best friends." She lifted her chin and shrugged her shoulders.

Avery smacked her playfully on the back. "I'll get it out of you one of these days. After a glass of wine," she called out as Libby walked away.

THERE WEREN'T TOO many days when Libby could just walk away from her job and obligations and do the one thing she loved besides running the café. She gathered all of her sketching supplies, packed a light lunch, and filled her backpack.

She set up her easel and had just sat down looking for inspiration when she heard a familiar voice. She looked up to see Harley wagging his tail and doing a little dance for Marshall.

It was a small town, and there were only a few places she could go to sketch without taking a car, but when she saw him, it reminded her that if she truly wanted some alone time, next time she'd take the car.

"What brings you here today?" She shielded her eyes from the sun as she locked gazes with him.

"I heard you were taking a day off, and I know you like this place."

Libby took in a deep breath and let it out slowly. "Yes. I'm just looking around for some inspiration." She turned her head and looked the other way.

He sat down on a grassy knoll and petted Harley. Libby sighed.

"Are you upset with me? Am I bothering you," he asked.

"No, and well, sort of. I came out here today because I want some time alone to be creative. I don't get to do it that often."

"And I messed that up for you. I see." He hung his head.

"Marshall, why are you really here?"

"Do you love Jackson?"

Libby knitted her brows tightly. "That's none of your business. I'm not going to discuss my personal life with you."

"I can't help it. I'm jealous."

"Jealous? Of what?"

"I thought maybe we felt something beyond employee and employer. That night —"

"That night was a mistake," she said, cutting him off. "I had too much wine to drink, and I told you that.

I was feeling lonely and vulnerable ... stupid, for sure." She glared at him.

"So kissing me would be stupid?" He stood up.

She looked up at him. "No, that's not what I meant. I mean, letting the wine take over my emotions. Listen, Marshall. I want to be your friend. That's it. Plain and simple. If you don't want that, then maybe you should leave the café. I'll give you a great recommendation. You don't have to worry about that."

"Sounds like you want me to go. Why didn't you fire me a long time ago?" His dark and cold stare sent shivers down Libby's arms and legs.

"I'm not going to rehash this with you. If you stay, then you need to be Blake's right hand man in the kitchen and forget about me, period. If you can't do that, then yes, you should go."

Marshall kicked a nearby stone and balled up his fists. "And so it shall be."

"Excuse me?" Libby tilted her head.

"I should have known I would never be good enough for you."

Marshall turned away and began walking down the gravel walkway.

"Marshall." Libby called out.

He stopped walking and paused a moment before turning back around. He dug his hands deep into his pockets and rocked back and forth on his feet. It appeared he was waiting her out.

Libby rose from her folding canvas stool and took a couple steps toward him. She stopped cold. Talking to him would be of no use. They'd already said everything there was to say. It was his decision and his alone.

"You have to find your happiness before you can share in love and happiness, Marshall." She blinked a couple of times as she studied his face from a distance.

He nodded. "I know. You've been a wonderful friend, and boss, Libby. I'll never forget you."

A small smile escaped her mouth. "You've been a great asset to the team."

Marshall turned on his heels and began to walk away.

Libby watched him go and didn't take her eyes off of him until she could no longer see him.

Avery was right about him. Libby couldn't fix his problems for him. He had to work that out on his own. Marshall had some serious baggage to unload and Libby, as strong and capable as she was, didn't have the time to help him heal and move forward. He'd have to find his own strength just like she did.

She took a few steps back toward her stool and canvas. She pulled in her bottom lip as her eyes moved from the stool to her blank canvas. She sighed. Libby wondered if this would be another missed opportunity to sketch. The thumping of Harley's wagging tail on the grass caught her attention. She reached over and patted him on the head.

"So much for a little peace and quiet," she mumbled under her breath.

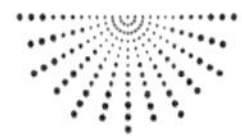

LIBBY WOKE up feeling as if she'd been hit by a runaway train. With bags under her eyes and a headache that wouldn't quit, she wandered into the kitchen to make some tea. Things always made more sense after a cup of tea. The kettle on the stove whistled, letting her know the water was ready. She went to the cupboard and looked over her tea selection. She made a mental note to get some more chamomile tea the next time she went shopping.

After about two sips of the piping hot tea, Libby realized what she needed was to get away for a bit— from the Seaside Café, the *Salty Dog*, and definitely Jackson and Marshall. She looked down at Harley, who was resting near her feet, and patted him gently on the head. She knew exactly what she needed to do. Pushing her chair out from the table, Libby made her way to the bedroom, where she packed an overnight bag. They were going to San Francisco. Libby would take Harley back to where they had both started.

Driving over the Golden Gate Bridge, Libby felt a sense of calmness. She'd always loved the city. It was Luke who had wanted to abandon the city and all they had created there together as a couple. Now a widow, Libby was trying to run two businesses and figure out her personal life as well. This was not at all what Luke or she had had in mind when they'd moved from the city.

Libby pulled up to the condominium. Fortunately for her, the renter had just moved out. Libby grabbed the small overnight bag and the two of them walked up to the door. Harley's tail started wagging, letting her know he was happy. He remembered it. The two of them entered the condo. Inside, it felt strange being back there. "So many memories of this place, Harley," Libby said.

After she had opened the windows to air the place out, Libby decided to take a walk. She was curious about whether Harley would remember any of their old stomping grounds. Their first stop was the park. It felt good to be back in the city and to see familiar places. She needed closure with Luke, the decisions they'd made, and the city they'd left behind.

LIBBY HAD CALLED up an old friend to set up a meeting. She was excited to see Alexandria. She realized while waiting for her, it had been way too long since she'd last seen her. With their busy schedules, Bodega might as well have been Seattle for distance. Making the time for visits was hard. Alexandria had promised to visit more often, but truthfully, the last time Libby had seen her had been at Luke's memorial service. She sighed. A lot had happened since they last saw each other.

Libby was a bit anxious about their meeting, but she knew Alexandria would give her the straight truth. They were old friends.

"Hello, Libby," Alexandria said as she slid her arms around her for a hug.

"It's great to see you. Thanks for seeing me on such short notice," Libby said.

"Not at all, Libby. You're a friend—a friend in need, too, it seems. Sit down. Let's talk about what you started telling me over the phone." Alexandria guided Libby over to the couch.

Libby opened up to Alexandria and poured her heart out. She told her every detail. After many tears and a box of tissues, Alexandria summarized the situation.

"You have a couple of options," she said as she wiped the tears from her friend's cheeks. "You can distance yourself from both of them, or you can distance yourself from just one. The choice is yours, Libby."

"I already made my choice. I told Marshall that all I wanted was friendship. I don't think he'll let that happen though. He wants more. He feels there's more."

"You might have to dismiss him if he continues with the aggressive behavior."

Alexandria made an excellent point. "I guess I need to tell Marshall to do some real soul-searching and hopefully he'll make the right decision to leave the café. I don't really want to fire him."

Alexandria nodded.

"What should I tell Jackson?" Libby asked.

"You have to decide, Libby. If you think it is more about you, which I suspect it is, then try to figure out if anything is stopping you from going all in with him. If you need to talk some more, I will always be here," she added as she got up from the couch.

"Thank you again for seeing me."

The two women walked toward the door. Alexandria leaned over and petted Harley on the head. "I'm glad to see ol' Harley is doing well, too."

Libby reached for the doorknob. She paused, turning toward Alexandria. "Why don't you come see me in Bodega? I would love for you to visit."

Alexandria nodded. "That sounds like a great idea. Then I can meet these two mysterious guys," she said, as the two of them giggled, going out the door.

Libby and Harley went back to the condo. She sat in an overstuffed chair and watched Harley as he slept. The city didn't hold the same feelings anymore. Sure she was excited about seeing the old place and all, but after she spent the afternoon there, all she could think about his her café, her friends, and her little cottage overlooking the bay.

Libby found she was anxious to get back to the café and see Avery. She missed her friends, and she missed her life in Bodega. It was finally time to sell the condo.

As she made the drive back, she vowed to see Sam more often, paint more, take more time off, and love life to the very fullest. It's what Luke would want her to do. And as for the new men in her life, she'd made that decision, too.

Libby returned home, and after a great night's rest,

she reported to work as usual. Avery, Blake, and some of the crew were busy getting things prepped for meal service. Libby jumped in to help.

"While I was driving back from San Francisco, I had an epiphany. I want to expand the café and add a small gift store to showcase my paintings and wind chimes," she said candidly.

"That's a great idea!" Avery said, nodding her head to the rest of the group showing her support.

Blake, getting the cue from his wife, nodded his agreement.

"I'm going to make an appointment with the bank tomorrow to discuss a construction loan. I'll keep you all posted," she said. Just then the wind chime to the front door of the café jingled, causing them all to turn their heads toward the door.

"Let me," she said to the staff.

She grabbed a menu and went flying around the corner to seat the customer, and there standing before her was none other than Jackson. She came to an abrupt halt staring right into his baby blues.

Talk about an awkward moment. Libby had been avoiding his calls since their night together. In fact, they hadn't spoken since he'd left her at her door almost a week ago. She cleared her throat and managed to exhale a half-hearted hello.

"I was hoping you could join me for a bowl of clam chowder."

"I don't know," she stammered.

Libby hadn't had time to rehearse what she was going to say to him the next time she saw him. She'd just gotten back from San Francisco, and although she'd made some decisions regarding her life, she wasn't quite ready to address them.

"I think they can work around you being gone from the kitchen for about a half hour. That's all the time I need," he said directly and with authority.

Libby nodded. Of all people, she didn't like games.

Having a serious discussion with Jackson was difficult. Libby found it distracting to stare into his lovely blue eyes remembering how it had felt to be in his arms, to be loved by him. She finally had to look down and away.

"I've missed you," he said.

"I've missed you, too," she said honestly. She raked her hand through her hair. "I needed a few days away, so I went to San Francisco—to the condo I shared with my husband."

"How was that?" he said, sounding a little uncertain.

"Good. I've decided to sell the condo."

He tilted his head and listened. "Are you sure about that decision?"

"Very sure. It once held a draw for me. For Luke and I. But my home is here, now."

"I see. Well that's a big decision. I know how you must have loved it."

"It was a hard decision, but the right one." She studied his face.

"Did you make any other decisions while there?" His dimples appeared as he smiled.

"Yes. Yes, I did. I'm going to expand the café and start selling my drawings and paintings. It's time for me to start living again. I'm ready." She reached across the table and laid her hands on his.

"Good. Now what about us?" He squeezed her hands.

"Us. That's a bigger decision. One I don't want to make lightly. But, I do feel something for you Jackson—something I want to explore."

CHAPTER ELEVEN

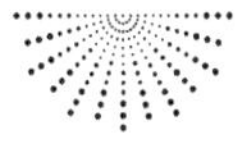

THAT EVENING, Libby showered with rose-scented bath gel. She made sure her legs and underarms were hair-free. She flossed and brushed her teeth—twice—and gargled with the special mouth rinse that was guaranteed to rid your mouth of bad breath for twelve hours. She went to her closet, opened the door, and turned on the light. She glanced from one end of the walk-in closet to the other. What would she wear? In the end, she decided on a pair of her bluest jeans and a cashmere pullover sweater in her favorite color, purple. She pulled out her black ankle boots and at the last minute chose a scarf that would complement her sweater. After she'd dressed, she gave herself a long look in the full-length mirror. Her hair looked great, her makeup just right. The only thing she wanted to add was white gold hoop earrings and a splash of her favorite cologne. Now the package was complete.

She'd told Jackson she'd drive herself over to his estate. She grabbed her purse and gave Harley a treat. Avery had promised to look in on him. She patted him on the head and told him to be a good boy, and out the door she went.

Once inside her car, she sighed. *I'm really doing this,* she said out loud. She turned on the radio, and before she knew it, she was driving up the long driveway to Jackson's home. She realized she had been gripping the steering wheel for the last few miles to his house. She wiped her moist palms on her jeans. She was nervous. She parked the car and gave herself a few moments to catch her breath and regain her composure. She saw the glow of lights through the windows—Jackson's windows. She'd really done it. She not only accepted the date, but she was also about to enter into it. She opened the car door and slid out of the seat.

"Here goes nothing, or here goes everything," she said to herself as she knocked on the big mahogany front door.

Jackson opened the door wide and motioned for her to step inside.

"You look beautiful tonight," he said softly.

Libby entered the long hallway and turned as he was closing the door.

"You look pretty handsome yourself."

"I just lit a fire. Dinner will be in a while. May I pour you a glass of wine, or make you a cocktail?" he asked softly.

Libby responded, "A glass of wine would be nice."

Jackson poured Libby a glass of wine, and he poured himself a glass of scotch. Music was playing softly in the background. The fire danced among the logs. The aroma of something delicious prepared by Jackson's staff drifted into the room, causing her tummy to growl.

This was the start of a perfect evening. They were sitting just inches apart, and Jackson reached over and gently placed his hand on hers. Libby stared into his eyes. The look she saw there sent shivers through her body. He reached for her, pulling her toward him engaging her trembling lips and evoking sensations she'd not soon forget.

Tantalized by his soft, full mouth, she gingerly accepted the full thrusts of his tongue. She moaned softly.

He put both his arms around her and began to run his hands up and down her back. She caressed his hair and his arms, but finally, after the most sensual kiss, he stopped.

Libby quickly regained her composure. "Is everything okay?" she asked. For a split second, it was like a scene replaying with Marshall in the camper.

"Of course, I just didn't want to go too far. Dinner will be ready soon, and we're not alone," he replied.

"Oh." Libby touched her lips, glad one of them had kept their head.

Even though the dinner was delicious, Libby had a hard time focusing on the food. Her stomach was tied up in a knot. All she could think about was Jackson's soft lips and what the remainder of the evening would hold.

After dinner, Jackson and Libby retreated to the room that had the fireplace. Jackson gave the staff the rest of the night off, so now it was just the two of them. Feeling a little more relaxed with the help of a couple of glasses of merlot, Libby sat down on the couch—the same couch where their passionate kiss had taken place earlier. Jackson settled in next to Libby, and the two of them stared at the flames dancing in and out of the logs. After a few minutes, mesmerized by the flames, Jackson sighed.

"What an excellent meal. I'm so glad you accepted my invitation. I think we fell off the track somehow on our last date. I couldn't understand why you wouldn't talk to me," he said as he reached over and touched her lightly on the hand.

"I know. I just needed some time. I should have explained that to you instead of making you wonder," Libby said, looking directly into his hungry eyes. "Forgive me?"

Jackson nodded. "No need to take full responsibility. How about three-fourths?" he said, laughing.

Libby jabbed him in the stomach. Just as she was pulling her hand back, Jackson grabbed it and kept it there. Then he pulled her arm so she would be closer to him. He reached up with his free hand and softly caressed her hair and touched her face. Then he leaned in and kissed her. They kissed for several minutes. Libby was thinking what a wonderful kisser he was when Jackson gently pushed Libby down on the couch and pulled himself up on top of her. Libby saw the desire in his eyes. Soon his hands were roaming her body.

Libby put up her hands against his chest. "No, I can't do this. I'm so sorry, Jackson."

Jackson sighed. He rolled off of her and sat back up. Libby straightened her clothes She ran her fingers through her hair, trying to put all the strands back in place. She picked up the wine glass from the table and took another sip. The silence was deafening. Finally after a few more seconds, Jackson spoke. "I thought this is what you wanted? What we wanted?"

"Yes, I do want this." Libby cradled her head in her hands. "I'm sorry about this. I don't know what is going on with me. I need to go have my head examined!" Libby said as she pushed herself up on the couch and headed down the hall to the bathroom. "I need a moment," she called out.

Once inside the bathroom, Libby took a couple of deep breaths. She'd kissed him before. They had done more than that during the fundraiser. *Why the cold feet now*, she wondered. She ran all the scenarios over in her mind again. Marshall was out. A definite out. She made the decision to sell the condo, and soon she'd sell the boat. She shouldn't be afraid of commitment. Luke would want her to move on. He would approve of Jackson, and she loved the way Jackson made her feel. His kisses alone were enough to entice her to go to bed with him again.

She brushed the few loose strands of hair back in place and looked long and hard at herself in the mirror. "You got this," she said out loud.

She emerged from the bathroom a different person. Strong, independent – the old Libby had resurfaced.

"I'm sorry I behaved like an idiot. I'm not really sure what came over me. I've got it together now. Where were we," she said pressing her lips to his.

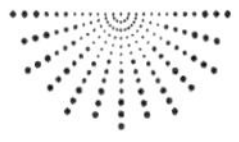

CHAPTER TWELVE

Monday morning at the café, Libby was flying high. Her night with Jackson proved to be monumental for them. She felt like she'd finally let go of the last piece holding them apart. She contacted a real estate agent and listed the condo. The next item on her agenda? Talk to Sam.

But first, Marshall. When he came into the café, he looked at Libby and then proceeded to walk back to the kitchen area. Libby watched him as he made his way toward the kitchen, presumably to clock in for his shift. *This is going to be awkward*, she thought to herself. "We're both adults here. Surely we can work together," she said under her breath.

For most of the day, Marshall did not engage in any eye contact, let alone any conversation with Libby.

During one of his breaks, he sat on the porch in one of the rocking chairs. Harley was sitting outside as well. Libby, knowing it would be difficult, gathered her composure and her resolve, then went outside to have a chat with him.

"Hey," she said to him as she took her place in the rocking chair next to him.

"Yes?" he snapped as he shot an icy glare her way. His look gave Libby chills that ran up her backside.

"Listen. Marshall, I want to be your friend, really I do," she began.

Marshall got up from the chair. He gazed out at the open spaces around the café. He casually turned toward Libby and with a constraint she could tell he didn't feel said, "I'm giving you my notice. I'll work until you can find someone else."

Relieved, Libby nodded in agreement.

"In fact, I can leave today if you'd like."

"No, that's not necessary, Marshall. You can stay till at least the end of the week."

"Please have my check ready for me at the end of my shift on Friday," he said, and then walked back inside.

The next couple of days were torture for everyone who worked there. The little café managed to avoid drama that often found its way into larger places. It felt strange, but the crew tried their best to act like nothing had happened. It was a difficult situation for everyone.

Libby had notified Jackson as to what was transpiring at the café.

"If Marshall is giving you a hard time, I can come out there—help you deal with him," Jackson said to her.

"He's got issues. I don't know what is really up with him. I know he's jealous."

"Jealous of what?"

"Us."

A quiet pause came after that.

"I mean, maybe he wishes things hadn't gone bad with his wife. He sees us getting close, and I think it just brought about some feelings." Libby said.

"I think the café will be better off without him," Jackson said.

Libby told herself that Marshall was upset and hurt and nothing more. But deep down, she wondered if he was truly capable of doing anything crazy. Maybe she should have had Jackson come by, but in the end, decided to not add him to an already volatile mix.

She just had to make it through one more day. Libby asked both Avery and Blake to stay until closing on Friday. She just wanted to ensure she wasn't alone when she handed Marshall his final check. She'd decided early on that she would put a little something extra in his check to tide him over until he found other employment.

The end of the day couldn't come soon enough for Libby. When the last customer had left, the crew began to clean the café, as they always did after closing. Marshall stayed until the very end. He was a great worker and truly an asset to her and the café. It was unfortunate it had to end this way.

At last, it was time to turn off the lights and lock the door. Avery, Blake, and Libby walked Marshall out. Marshall turned around and went down the line, shaking their hands and thanking them. When he got to Libby, he held her hand for just a bit longer.

Libby cleared her throat. "Your final check from the Seaside Café," she said as she handed him the envelope. "I put a little something extra in there to tide you over until you find another job. If you need a reference, please don't hesitate to give my name and number," she added.

The silence was very strange. Marshall didn't comment on the extra money she gave him or the offer of a reference. He just stared at her, his jaw tightening so everyone could see his anger. Finally, after a few seconds that seemed more like several minutes had passed, he spoke. "My past is muddy with secrets and lies. My wife never abused me. I abused her. I never laid a hand on her, but I will forever be ashamed of the verbal and mental abuse she endured," Marshall said, lowering his head to hide his eyes.

The three of them gasped. All this time, they'd thought he was running from the abuse he'd suffered at the hands of his wife, only to find out that the opposite was true.

"Who are you?" Libby asked.

"I owned a chain of well-known home décor stores."

They weren't sure if they had heard him correctly. "Home décor stores?" Avery blurted.

Marshall nodded his head. "At one time, I was a wealthy man. I lost it all because I loved alcohol more than I loved my wife or myself. I was an abusive husband and employer, and in the end, I lost everything that was ever important to me. I've had to live with the fact that I took not only my own happiness and threw it away, but I also destroyed others' happiness as well. It's something I'll have to live with for the rest of my life."

Libby, hating the awkwardness of the entire situation, spoke up. "Marshall, I'm glad you've finally come clean with us and, more importantly, that you are sober. It's an illness, a disease, and it can destroy lives. I'm sorry you couldn't tell us, your friends, so we could have helped you on your journey. It's what stood in the way of us developing a deeper relationship. Your whole persona has been a lie. How could you do that to us?" she asked, shaking her head.

"I don't begrudge you wanting to keep some of it private, but to not share it with us after all this time—it's difficult to absorb. I wish you all the happiness as you embark on your journey to wellness. There's just not sure there is a place for you here given all the secrets you've kept. I hope as you search for happiness, you'll have a sense of freedom to share your story. You'll be happier if you do."

He turned and walked away. The three of them watched as he made his way off the porch and down the sidewalk. Stunned by what had just occurred and not able to process it, one by one, they stumbled and searched for words. Just as Libby was about to speak, Marshall stopped, turned around, and mouthed the words, "I'm sorry."

Libby, feeling terrible about how things had ended, rushed up to him. "Marshall, if there's anything we can do for you, please don't hesitate to ask. If we can help you, we will."

Marshall moved away from her with his head hung low. "I'll be in touch," he said, and he turned back around and walked into the evening mist and fog that was so customary in Bodega.

"Well, talk about surprise endings," Blake announced.

Avery nodded in agreement.

"That explains why I never saw him with a glass of wine. Now that I think about it, he always had another beverage when I was drinking wine," Libby said as she walked to the back of the café to get her things.

Blake and Avery watched in silence. "Poor Libby," Avery whispered to Blake, as he hugged her.

"Come here, Libby. Time for a group hug," Avery said, gesturing.

"Given the circumstances, we're walking you home, Libby," Blake said as the three of them exited the Seaside Café.

Libby didn't even argue. She was exhausted.

CHAPTER THIRTEEN

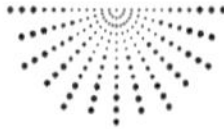

THE NEXT COUPLE of days were tough on Libby. She knew she had done the right thing by letting Marshall go. At first, she thought she'd felt something for him, but as time went on, she realized it was empathy more than anything else. Jackson was the one who stirred deep feelings and yearning inside her—the things essential to a good romantic relationship. Libby, determined to find out if Jackson was indeed the right choice, picked up the phone and called him.

LIBBY COULDN'T UNDERSTAND why she felt so nervous about going out with Jackson. This was not their first date. She must have looked through her closet a zillion times before settling on jeans and a long-sleeved blouse. It was fall out on the coast, and nights could be chilly, so she found a lovely scarf to accentuate her outfit. She sat on the couch petting Harley, waiting for Jackson to arrive.

"Harley, boy, I don't know why I have butterflies in my stomach, but I do."

Harley just looked up at Libby with his soft brown eyes. Libby smiled. There was a knock at the door, and Libby knew it was Jackson. Harley and Libby went to the door, both eager to see him.

"Hi," she said to him, smiling from ear to ear and with a sparkle in her eyes. "Please come in."

"You look beautiful," he said, walking into the main area of her house. "Are you ready to go?"

She nodded as she opened the hall closet to get out her leather jacket. "Harley, you be a good boy. See you in a couple of hours," she said as she patted him on the head.

Driving to the restaurant was quiet except for the radio that was turned down low. Country music playing softly in the background and road noise were the only sounds surrounding them.

Jackson cleared his throat. "I hope you like prime rib. I'm taking you to this little restaurant that's famous for it. The atmosphere is low-key, and there's a nice big fireplace in a small dining room. I think you'll like it."

"Yes, I do like prime rib, and the restaurant sounds delightful," she said, smiling at him in the dark.

"It's a bit of a drive, though, about forty-five minutes, but worth every minute."

"That's great," she said. "I love to drive these back roads. It does get dark early, though, and there're lots of deer, cows, and other wildlife, so do be careful."

Gripping the wheel Jackson concentrated on the road.

"Of course, I'll be careful," he said tentatively.

He reached over and took her hand. Immediately, Libby felt goose bumps traveling up her arm and down her leg, and she ending up feeling a bit like a schoolgirl on a first date. She giggled a little and got Jackson's attention. "I'm just feeling so happy to be with you. I know it took us some time to get to this place, and I'm so glad you waited for me," she added, squeezing his hand gently and then rubbing the outside of his thumb with her own.

Jackson slowed the truck down and pulled over off onto the shoulder.

"What are you doing?" Libby asked.

Jackson put the truck in park and then pulled her toward him. Libby didn't stop him. They were about two inches apart, and she could feel his warm breath on her face. They didn't speak any words; they just looked into each other's eyes.

"You are one beautiful lady." He pulled her closer until their lips touched. He softly caressed her shoulders. She put her arms around him, and soon they were kissing. He gently parted her lips, and the kiss deepened. The kiss only lasted a few seconds, but it would remain on both of their minds for a very long time.

"Well, look at us acting like a couple of kids." He laughed. "Guess we should continue on to the restaurant?" Jackson asked.

Libby couldn't speak, so she just nodded her head. Food really wasn't what was on her mind right now, but she would play along for a while.

CHAPTER FOURTEEN

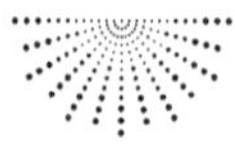

THEY ARRIVED at the quaint restaurant. Jackson quickly peered at his watch.

"I hope they didn't give our table away. The little delay put us a few minutes off our reservation time. But it was worth it," he added as he gave her a quick peck on the cheek.

Libby smiled. He got out of the truck and ran around to the passenger side to help her out. When he reached in to take her hand, he held hers for a few seconds, causing an array of feelings to spread through her body like a wildfire out of control.

"Libby, I'm so sorry if I rushed you—"

"Shh," Libby said as she put her finger to his lips. "It's all good. *We're* good." And with that last word, she took her finger away from his mouth and replaced it with her lips. They both gave a little groan, and then Libby said, "We'd better get inside, or they really will give our table away, and I'm hungry!"

Dinner was delicious, just as Jackson had promised. The atmosphere was intimate and warm. They dined on prime rib, mashed potatoes, and asparagus. For dessert, they had cheesecake. They sipped on cabernet sauvignon, and after her second glass, Libby knew she would be as giddy as a college freshman.

The ride back to town was enchanted. They listened to the radio, and with every romantic song, the caressing of body parts began. First their hands, then their arms, and occasionally Libby would slide her hand up and down Jackson's firm thigh. He would reciprocate, and it gave Libby goose bumps and chills running down to her toes.

Jackson waited patiently for the invitation. It didn't take long. They'd just pulled up to the house when Libby leaned close and whispered, "Please come in for a bit."

Inside, Jackson patted Harley on the head and proceeded to make his way to the couch. Libby went into the bedroom to put her purse away. She quickly looked around to be sure nothing was out of place in the bedroom in case the two of them ended up there tonight. She wondered if it was the wine making all the plans for her, or was it just helping her to do what she really wanted to?

Libby joined Jackson on the couch. Over the course of the evening they'd discussed her expansion ideas.

"I think it's a very good idea that you're expanding the café. Wind chimes are always a great souvenir for tourists, and to showcase your artwork, too, is a bonus," Jackson said proudly. "You know, I have had my eye on Bodega for quite some time," he added.

Libby nodded.

"What'd you say we join forces?"

"How so?"

"I'll open a small tasting room inside your gift store."

"That's a great idea, Jackson."

"I think our collaborating would be a genius idea," he said.

Libby thought about it a second. His wines could bring in more customers, and that would be good for her and the café. "I'm all in if you are," Libby said excitedly.

"Well," Jackson started, "it could work. Yes, I think it really could." He took both of Libby's hands into his own. "But are you sure you want to invest your future and your livelihood with me?" Jackson asked as he held onto her hands and looked deeply into her eyes.

"Yes, I do. I want to do this with you. It will be so great to blend our interests as well as grow our relationship."

"Yes," they both said in unison and kissed to seal the deal.

Libby drew back after a brief moment. Staring into Jackson's eyes, she asked him directly about a contract. "I know you have your money, property, and the like, and I have the café." She almost spilled the beans by mentioning the *Salty Dog*, but decided the time wasn't right. "I just think to protect all of our interests we should have something drawn up," she continued.

Jackson looked deeply into her eyes. She felt a little restless. She wasn't sure if she had offended him. "Of course. Let's get our lawyers to draw something up that makes us both happy," he murmured.

Libby knew they would not need to discuss this sensitive subject again. They would each tell their prospective lawyers what to draw up, each would sign, and that would be the end of the discussion.

He reached over and moved a tendril of her hair and placed it behind her ear. She focused on his face, his plump lips, square jawline, and dimples. She lightly swept her tongue across her lips. He pulled her in embracing her as he devoured her lips. She softly moaned. She wrapped her arms around his neck holding tight as they kissed. She pulled back momentarily and gazed into his hungry eyes. Her hands were trembling and knots were forming deep in the pit of her stomach.

Libby pulled herself together. "Stay with me," she whispered into his ear.

"Are you sure you're ready," he said tenderly. "This was where you and Luke …"

In answer, Libby stood and led him to her bedroom.

They slowly undressed each other, taking the time to be sensitive to the next actions they were about to indulge in. Jackson kissed her, then ran his kisses down her neck and across her shoulder. The kisses were soft, but Libby could sense the pent-up need he had—that they both had.

Jackson lifted her onto the king-size bed and joined her, cradling her head as he kissed her passionately, caressing the entire length of her body. There, in the throes of pure passion, Jackson and Libby forever changed the course of their relationship.

THE EXPANSION of the café began as planned. Libby and the crew were excited about all the possibilities this new venture would bring, not only to Bodega but also to each other. Mrs. Johnson, Hunter, and Tony would all get extra hours. She hadn't decided exactly how it would all pan out, but she knew she would need someone to run the gift store portion and also help with the art gallery. Jackson said he would take care of the hiring of a sommelier.

The mood couldn't have been more festive at the Seaside Café. Avery, Blake, and the entire staff were bursting with joy. They were happy to be working, pleased to be working for Libby, and most of all, happy for her.

Libby realized the next step in their relationship would be to introduce Jackson to Sam and give Jackson a tour of the *Salty Dog*. That was going to be the ultimate test of her strength. She knew the *Salty Dog* had been Luke's baby and bringing another man to the boat would be the crucial piece to the puzzle of letting her old life go and beginning anew.

Libby had time to spare so she headed down to the docks and waited. It gave her time to collect her thoughts. She watched as he tied her to the posts, and then she made her way in front of the boat. One by one, the hired hands came flying off the bow of the *Salty Dog*. Libby clasped her hands and held them in front until she saw Sam.

"Hi, Sam," she called out.

Sam looked up. "Hi, Libby! What are you doing here—everything all right at the café?" He jumped down off the boat and walked toward her.

"Yes, everything is just fine. I just wanted to talk to you for a few minutes."

Libby told Sam about the expansion of the café and her idea about selling wind chimes and displaying her art. He nodded while smiling, being careful not to interrupt her.

Then she dropped the bomb she'd been holding back regarding Jackson. Sam listened intently.

After a few minutes, Sam said, "I have to digest this a bit. You've really laid it on me," he said, chuckling. "Let me see if I got this right. You're expanding the café, you have a new boyfriend, and you think you're in love?"

"All of the above and guilty as charged," Libby laughed.

"Sounds like you've got it all under control, Libby. But most important, you sound happy. You've got my blessing. What else do you need?"

"I'd like to give Jackson a tour of the boat. Maybe even take him out for a ride. I think it's important he see the life I had with Luke so that he will understand me even more," she said.

Sam nodded. "No problem. Just let me know when. I'll make sure we're ready."

"Thank you, Sam. I don't even know for sure that he likes the ocean, or boats for that matter."

"I guess you'll find out." Sam chuckled.

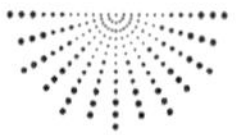

THE CONSTRUCTION of the gift shop was coming along well. Libby and Avery were purchasing the finishing touches for the space, and Jackson was getting his end of the business together, too. They had tentatively set the opening date in two weeks' time. There was a lot to do still, but Libby was up for the challenge. She decided she didn't want to take Jackson out to the *Salty Dog* until after the shop opened. One thing at a time.

The day of the grand opening was a big deal in Bodega. Everyone loved Libby and her friends, and they wanted her to succeed. The outpouring of love would forever be etched in her mind.

She had sold five wind chimes within the first hour of opening and one of her art pieces by the end of the day. Jackson sold two cases of his best wine, some wine glasses, and other wine paraphernalia.

The grand opening was a success. Libby and Jackson celebrated with a nice quiet evening at her place.

"What a great day!" Libby said as they touched wine glasses.

"I think we're going to have a lot of those," Jackson replied. He leaned over and gave Libby a long, warm kiss. She melted into his arms. They kissed for a few moments, and then she gently pulled back.

"Jackson. There's something I need to tell you."

"Oh, no. More stuff you have to come clean about?" he said, chuckling.

She nodded.

"Okay, let's have it. I think we're strong enough to handle any hiccups."

"You know I was married and that my husband died."

He nodded.

"I never told you how he died."

"I figured you'd tell me when you felt the time was right," Jackson said lovingly.

"Well, the time is right," Libby said.

Libby explained everything to Jackson. She started from the beginning. How she and Luke had met in San

Francisco—his dream, and how they'd followed it to Bodega. She went on to tell him all about Sam and how if it weren't for him, she'd be broke.

"I'd like to take you out to the docks so you can meet Sam and see the *Salty Dog*."

"I'd love that, Libby. Can I ask you a question?"

"Sure," Libby said.

"How did you all come up with the name of the boat?"

Libby chuckled. She imagined Luke looking down at her at this very moment. He'd loved telling the story of how the boat got her name.

Libby began. "When Luke was in college, he tended bar. One of his specialty drinks was the salty dog. He made those drinks with a twist, though. He added a little maraschino cherry juice. Some people christen their boats with champagne. We drank salty dog cocktails. It was just an inside joke."

Jackson nodded. "Well, I didn't know if it had something to do with Harley or a cocktail," he laughed.

Libby gasped. "Harley did jump overboard before and also slipped off into the water. So I guess you could say he's a salty dog, too." They both laughed, picturing Harley jumping into the ocean.

CHAPTER SIXTEEN

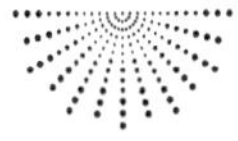

LIBBY AWOKE to the sun shining through her window. She lay in bed for a few moments, taking in the rays. Harley was being quiet this morning, and she decided to take full advantage of staying in bed for a few more moments.

Today was going to be a big day. She and Jackson were driving to the docks so he could meet Sam and take a sail on the *Salty Dog.* Libby felt like nothing could go wrong now. Everything was coming together. The café was operating in the green, and the *Salty Dog* was, too. The gift store was doing well, considering it had only been open a short time. Libby smiled.

Harley came up to the side of the bed. Libby could sense he was standing there. She ignored him for a few seconds, knowing he would not go away. All of a sudden, he moaned and groaned and nudged the bed with his nose.

"Okay, boy. I'm getting up. I know … you're hungry," she said as she climbed out of bed. Petting Harley on the head and slipping her feet into her nearby slippers, Libby shuffled to the kitchen to feed Harley and get the coffee started.

Libby gathered her sketch pad and pencils. She packed a light lunch and waited patiently for Jackson. The clock said ten. Jackson was supposed to pick her up at nine forty-five. Libby started getting an awful feeling. She wondered if he had reconsidered the offer. If that was the case, why wouldn't he call her and just say so? Her mind was running away with its thoughts now. She imagined all kinds of negative things. Just as she was getting herself all worked up, there was a light knock on the door. Libby rushed and pulled it open. There stood Jackson, dressed in boating attire.

"You're late."

"Yes, sorry about that. Had a few loose ends to tie up at the estate," he said as he entered her place. "I tried to call, but the coverage out here along the coast isn't consistent."

"I'm glad you're here, now." She gave him a peck on the cheek.

Jackson knew where the leash was, so he went to get

it. Libby grabbed her stuff and the lunch, and the three of them walked out of the house.

Jackson pulled into the lot adjacent to the docks and unloaded the car. The two started off for the short walk to the boat with Harley picking up the rear.

"Hello, Sam," Libby greeted.

Sam smiled and threw up a big welcoming wave. "Welcome aboard the *Salty Dog*," he said proudly.

Libby made the introductions, and then while Sam was getting things ready for push off, Libby gave Jackson the five-cent tour of the boat. They both went down into the berth so she could put some things away.

"It's cozy down here," Jackson commented.

Libby nodded. "I usually stay up top. It's hard to enjoy the view from down here," she added.

"I think it could get a little stuffy down here." Jackson wrinkled his nose.

Within a few moments, Sam had cast them off into the deep blue. The *Salty Dog* spat and jolted her way deeper into the waters, the waves hitting the bow. Libby couldn't help but notice Jackson had an edgy look about him. After a few minutes, she asked him if he was okay.

"Just haven't been on a boat in this kind of water before," he said through clenched teeth.

"Have you ever been on a boat before, at all?" Libby asked.

"Yes. On a lake," he quipped.

Libby grimaced. "This could turn out to be torture for you instead of pleasure." Libby moved toward Sam. She was about to make an executive decision and have Sam turn the *Salty Dog* around to head back to Bodega.

Jackson, sensing that was exactly what she was about to do, intervened. "I'll be all right. Let's not cancel the trip prematurely. I want to see if I can handle it."

"I don't want you to hate the experience, Jackson."

He nodded, letting her know he was appreciative of her concern.

After about twenty minutes of motoring out, Jackson saw a school of dolphins playing ahead of them. "Look over there," he shouted as he pointed.

Libby smiled. The wonders of the ocean never ceased to amaze her. The further they motored out, the calmer the water became, giving Jackson a chance to breathe and enjoy his surroundings. Libby, sensing the change, took the opportunity to get her sketch pad out. Jackson walked back to where Sam was steering, and soon it appeared that Jackson got over his uneasiness of boats out on the ocean. She looked up from her sketching when she heard laughter and Harley barking.

After about an hour, Jackson approached her, saying he was getting hungry. "Oh, gosh, Jackson, I totally forgot about our lunch. Let me go get the basket from the berth. How much further, Sam?" Libby called out as she fetched the basket from down below.

"Just around this bend we should be able to stop," he called out.

Luke and Sam had scouted many inlets, coves, and harbors in the area.

"You're going to love this place," Libby grinned.

Sam shut the motor off, and the *Salty Dog* coasted into a soft area that had a homemade dock. Sam jumped off the boat and carried the rope with him, securely tying her up to a post. He reached out his hand to help Libby out of the ship first, and Jackson followed. Harley had run ahead of them all. The three of them walked up a small grassy knoll. On the other side was a lagoon with a sandy beach with driftwood and shells strewn all about from the tides, and various vegetation.

"Wow! What a gorgeous view," Jackson gasped. "This makes up for the slight reservations I had about coming."

Libby nodded. It did for her, too. She never got that excited about fishing on the boat, but day trips to places as exotic as this little private beach always made up for her not wanting to go.

The three of them walked a little farther and found a place where they could lay out a blanket. They dined on fried chicken and potato salad, all the while enjoying the scents and sounds of the bay. In the distance, the vibrant green hills covered with yellow mustard and lavender plants provided a natural canvas of color and smells.

Libby looked at the two guys as they ate, talked, and joked, and she knew she'd made the right choice. Jackson was thoughtful and caring, and he was everything Luke would want in a man for her. She was convinced of that. Yes, it was a beautiful day in Bodega, and her life was about to change once more.

CHAPTER SEVENTEEN

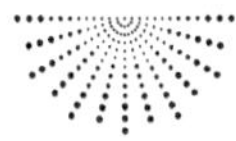

JACKSON COULDN'T STOP TALKING about the trip out on the boat. He was fascinated with everything, and he wanted to talk about it—a lot. "The waves were coming in the front of the vessel," he said excitedly.

"The bow. The waves came over the bow," Libby corrected.

He nodded, and then repeated, "The bow. Sam took control of the steering, and it was evident he knew what he was doing."

Libby nodded. "Yes, he knows every inch of the *Salty Dog*."

"I know it has to be difficult every time you set foot on that boat, but I'll always be there for you, Libby." He leaned in and kissed her, and Libby melted into his kiss and his arms for the rest of the night.

The next morning over coffee and sweet rolls, Libby and Jackson teased each other all morning with soft, wet kisses and romantic touches.

With the weight of the *Salty Dog* mystery now lifted off Libby's shoulders, she had more time and energy to spend on the café and the recently opened gift store. Unfortunately, working the long hours did nothing but add undue stress and fatigue to Jackson's and her relationship.

Libby was worn out from running the café and the gift shop. Mrs. Johnson and the gang helped out when and where they could, but with school in session, Hunter and Anthony could only work certain hours, and Mrs. Johnson had recently become a grandmother and wanted to, understandably, spend time with her new grandbaby. Avery and Blake were already spread thin, leaving Libby to pick up the slack.

Jackson had not spent much time in Bodega because he was busy at his estate. He'd hired a young woman to help with the wine tasting side, and she was working out rather well. However, the gift shop had become increasingly busy and Libby decided she'd discuss hiring more help with Jackson. She also wanted to talk to him about all the trips she was making to the Jackson Keys estate. All the traveling back and forth was getting old.

After a long day at the café, Libby decided she would take a warm bubble bath and treat herself to a glass of Jackson Keys Estate merlot. She'd only been in the tub for a few minutes when the phone rang. Reaching over to grab the cordless phone and dripping bubbles all across the floor, she managed to answer it without dropping it into the tub.

"Hello," she said.

"Hi, babe!"

"I'm just soaking in a tub full of hot water and bubbles," she whispered suggestively.

"I like the sound of that," he teased. "I know working all those hours has got to be wearing you out. I know it's wearing me out with all the travel back and forth."

"Agreed. But I don't know what the solution is."

"Well, I have a couple of ideas. We can talk about it more when I come for my next visit."

Libby sighed. "That can't come soon enough."

Libby was happy to see Jackson. They'd been pretty busy running the businesses and hadn't had as much time together. She was hoping she would get him alone. Maybe she could convince him to stay over.

The lunch crowd had formed and the café bustled with normal chatter.

"When you have a break, let's go for a walk," Jackson said as he poured his own ice water from the pitcher. "By the way, hello, and don't you look lovely," he added.

"Glad you added that last part or I would have been upset," she said, chuckling. Libby walked back into the kitchen, did a quick assessment, and determined that the crew was doing just fine.

"I could probably go for that walk now. Avery, Blake, and Anthony have it covered in the kitchen," she concluded.

The two of them and Harley took a walk. The town was only one street long where various businesses dotted one side of the street. Houses lined the opposite side. It was a quaint village, and Libby really had grown to appreciate it. Jackson liked Bodega, too. He'd felt it was the right move for his entrepreneurial venture, but he enjoyed living in wine country with the rolling hills and the landscape of vines, too.

Jackson took in a deep breath. "Ahh, the freshness of the coast." We have the best of both worlds. The rich aroma of ripening grapes and the fresh smells of the ocean."

Libby nodded.

"How could anyone give one or the other up?" Jackson said.

"I could never give up living here …" Libby furrowed her brows. "Wait a minute. Did I just walk into a trap?" She stopped walking and let go of his hand.

Jackson cleared his throat. "I've wanted to discuss our long-distance relationship," he muttered.

"It's not really long distance," Libby corrected him. "You live only about an hour from me," she said, puzzled.

"Well, that's on a good day. It can take up to an hour and a half with traffic and unexpected delays," he offered. "With the harvest, I've been so busy at the estate. That's made my trips here scarce." He took her hand. "I miss you."

"Okay, where exactly are you going with this?" she asked him pointedly.

They looked at each other, one waiting for the other to speak first.

Finally, Jackson started. "You know I care about you deeply. We've come so far in our relationship. We have trust, faith, and a business together, and I can't think of anything that has made me as happy for a very long time. But, I'm tired of all the commuting back and forth, and I would love to just come here once in a while."

Libby gasped.

"No, it's not what you think. I want *us* to come to Bodega once in a while," he added quietly as he looked for some reaction from her.

"You want me to leave Bodega? Leave the café, the gift store, and the *Salty Dog* and move in with you … at the estate?"

Jackson nodded his head.

A million thoughts and emotions rushed in at once. This all seemed so familiar. Luke had asked her to leave everything she loved and move away with him, too. "I have to think about that, Jackson. That is a huge step for me."

He nodded again. "I understand."

"Maybe we should sell all the businesses and properties and start new—build something together that's ours?" she said eagerly.

"I could never sell the estate, Libby. That property has been in my family for a long time. My family built that winery with years of blood, sweat, and tears."

"I know, Jackson. I'm just grasping at ideas right now. I'm worn out on most days from working the café and the store. I'm not sure how much longer I can sustain things alone. I thought about hiring more personnel." She hesitated, then added, "Maybe I just need to sell the place," she said, but in her heart, she knew she didn't want to give up what she'd worked so hard for here.

"I don't want you to do anything you'd regret or eventually become bitter over. Let's both sleep on it," he said as he pulled her close to him. "I love you, Libby."

Libby hugged and then kissed him. She loved him, too.

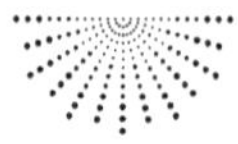

LIBBY HAD a lot of soul-searching to do regarding the quandary Jackson had posed to her regarding their living arrangements. She loved Bodega, but it was more Luke's and her town than Jackson's and hers, so she understood how awkward that must be for Jackson. Maybe he was right. It was time for a change.

One thing Luke had taught her was that life was a gamble. They'd risked their life savings to buy the *Salty Dog*, and it had turned out all right. Except for losing him, which no one could possibly have predicted, the *Salty Dog* did just what he'd said it would do. It paid the bills, it continued to bring happiness to those who cruised aboard her out into the deepest waters, and it caught hundreds of pounds of fish daily. Libby sighed. Thinking about all she'd been through over the past three years weighed heavily on her.

Libby got to the café and immediately went to the kitchen. "Can I have your attention, guys?"

Startled by Libby's direct approach, Avery and Blake turned around to see what all the fuss was about.

"Sure, boss. What's up?" Avery asked, with a puzzled look on her face.

Libby began to tell them how Jackson had approached her with an idea of changing their living arrangements. He was tired of commuting and not spending time at his estate. She told them she was getting weary of all the hours spent running the café, and now the gift store. Avery and Blake glanced at each other trying to figure out what Libby was attempting to tell them. In the middle of her telling her friends the story, it occurred to her that she really didn't know what the plans were, but the solution was relatively straightforward. He wanted her to move to the estate.

"What are you going to do, Libby?" Avery asked.

Libby wished she knew.

That evening, with a glass of wine in her hand, Libby made the call. She couldn't put it off any longer. She punched his number into the phone, but once she heard his voice, she froze. The hairs on her arms stood straight up and a shiver ran down her back.

"Hi there," he said. "This is an unexpected but wonderful surprise. Is everything okay?"

"I was telling Avery and Blake about our conversation, and it suddenly occurred to me that I wasn't sure what we were going to be doing," Libby acknowledged softly. "I really want to make this work, Jackson. I can't say goodbye to you, but I'm not ready to say goodbye to Bodega either."

"Do you feel comfortable with Blake and Avery running things at the café and with you checking in on them from time to time?" he asked.

Libby thought about the notion of Avery and Blake taking on the tremendous responsibility. "That's putting a lot of responsibility on them. Maybe I should just sell it," she said, but her heart dropped at the thought "I bet I wouldn't have any trouble selling it. It has a high-profit record. In fact, Avery and Blake might be interested."

"After we just expanded, I'm not sure that would be wise," Jackson said. "But you could offer them the chance to purchase half of the business and be co-owners. That way you could still maintain some control."

Libby liked the sound of that.

"If and when you decide to sell your half, you could offer it to them then."

Her excitement began to build. This could work. "What about the wine tasting bar?" Libby asked.

"I'd like to keep that separate for now. It has my family name and logo. We could set it up as a lease option, and that way I could renew it or not."

Libby loved that idea, too. "You're sure you want me and Harley to come live with you full-time, Jackson?"

"I have never been more certain," he murmured into the receiver.

"I made another big decision today," she said. "I really made it a long time ago, but I'm actually going to do something about it now." Libby said.

"Oh?"

"I'm selling The Salty Dog."

"Are you sure, Libby? I want you to be absolutely sure that's what you want to do."

"I've never been surer. I met with Sam. He's going to get a loan. I don't want to make any profit from her, just cut my ties and let him have her. You should have seen the smile on his face. He's a different Sam these days."

"I'm glad. He's the perfect person to captain her." He paused then added, "Listen, Libby. Remember when you felt as if you needed to get something off your chest regarding the news story you saw about me?"

"Yes."

"I have something I need to tell you," he began.

Libby listened intently.

"There's another reason I don't like the long drives between your place and mine. A very long time ago, I had someone special in my life. She was taken from me suddenly, like Luke was taken from you. My life has been in turmoil since—until I met you, that is."

"Was it a boating accident?" Libby asked.

"No, it was a car accident. She also lived on the coast, in a small village about twenty miles up the road from you. She drove back and forth on most weekends to visit me. On a cold, rainy, winter night, she was traveling on the road, and as she went around a bend, a deer ran out in front of her. She hit her brakes, swerved, and went over an embankment."

"Oh, Jackson. That's awful." When he didn't speak, she added, "So that's why you don't want us to travel back and forth while we nurture our long-distance relationship."

"Yes, that's part of it. The other part of it is that life is too short. You and I know that, perhaps better than most. We have to grab on to all the opportunities life sends us, both in love and in life. I don't want you to get away. I want to spend the rest of my life with you, Libby." There—he said it; all of it. Now he would wait for her response.

He paused as if waiting for her response. "You're right, Jackson. Life is too short. I guess we both found that out the hard way. I think we make a great team, and I would love to be your partner in both love and life. I wish I were there with your arms around me."

"I wish you were here, too," he said. "I can't wait to get you into my bed. I'm going to make sweet love to you like never before."

"Ooh. I love the sound of that," she whispered

LIBBY AND JACKSON had their respective lawyers draw up the proposal and then met with Avery and Blake to discuss it. They loved the idea and were excited about the prospect of being co-owners of the Seaside Café. Libby and Jackson kept the quaint cottage overlooking the bay. They would need a place to stay when visiting, but they'd decided to have it renovated to suit both their tastes. Libby was excited about the new life she would soon embark on. She would have to learn about the wine business, something she was eager to do.

It would be difficult to say goodbye to Sam and the

gang. It was especially going to be hard to say goodbye to Avery. She had been Libby's confidante and friend for the last few years. Libby always knew she could confide in her, and Avery would tell her the truth, even if it wasn't comfortable.

On Libby's last day, Jackson drove to Bodega to get her and Harley. "Are you ready to go?"

"I am," she responded matter-of-factly. She'd come to terms with leaving, and it wasn't as painful as she thought it would be. She knew it wasn't a goodbye, but more of a see you later. She'd be back soon.

"Okay then, let's go," Jackson said as the three of them walked out of the cottage, locking the door behind them. Libby turned around one last time as they made their way down the sidewalk toward Jackson's truck. She stared hard at the little seaside cottage with its weather-beaten siding, vivid blue door and shutters, and let out a long sigh. She looked back at Jackson. He shoved his hands deep in his pockets. He'd give her as much time as she needed. She spun around and gave one final look at the place she'd called home, then she slowly turned back toward Jackson and started walking slowly at first then picking up her pace as she got closer.

He removed his hands from his pockets and opened his arms wide. She leaped into his arms, and he twirled her around and around. She kicked back her heels and held on as she found his mouth and kissed him. He put her down but they remained embraced. They stood for a moment enjoying the moment. She reached out and cupped his face with her hands. She gently bit her bottom lip as she thought about what she was going to say. In the end, she just said three little words. The most powerful words ever spoken. "I love you."

EPILOGUE

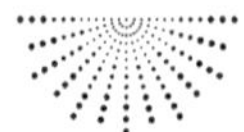

NOTHING GOOD CAME EASY. That was another famous and wise expression Libby had learned early on. And it was true. From the moment Luke and she had left their cozy condo in the city, to purchasing the boat and then the café, to the sad reality that Luke would never be coming back, Libby had had to dig deep and show she was the strong woman she and Luke both knew she was. It didn't mean it came without sacrifice or sorrow, or self-doubt. Because it was all of that and more. But Libby knew that if she was to be successful, she'd have to let some of the baggage go. It was the hardest part of going on without him. Jackson was patient, thoughtful, and kind. She would need all of his love as she weathered the emotions that came crashing down from time to time.

Avery and Blake took care of the café as if it was their very own. It meant the world to Libby to have friends and colleagues she could put so much faith in and not be disappointed. Libby discovered through her weekly phone conversations with Avery that every now and then Marshall would stop by for a cup of chowder, as would Sam. That always brought a smile to her face. She was learning the wine business at a hurried pace. Once she was in, she was all in. Jackson loved that about her. They were true partners in every sense of the word.

Once in a while, she'd stop and think about how everything had started and how everything had turned out. She would have never been able to predict what would happen or the sorrow she'd felt deep in her heart from losing the love of her life. But Jackson, her dear beloved Jackson, made it easy for her to live and love again.

I hope you enjoyed The Salty Dog. I've included the first chapter from Ties That Bind a story inspired by true events.

Debbie

PROLOGUE

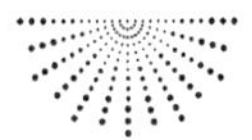

I ALWAYS SAID my life began when I met Charles. He made everything better. We had a great life together, and despite my dysfunctional childhood, I'd say my life turned out pretty good. Sometimes, when I'd think back about all I'd been through, I'd shake my head in disbelief. It was hard for even me to believe some of the things I'd been through and discovered. It took me years to finally talk about it openly but once I did, closing those floodgates was next to impossible.

Those memories blazed brightly and were sometimes hard to put aside. So, I started keeping a journal in the hopes of writing my whole story someday. Like most people, time got away from me. I was thankful that Carole became interested in documenting my story.

Even though Charles was interested, there came a time when he felt it was water under the bridge and time to move forward. I told myself the same thing, but sometimes it's harder to do than you'd think.

When Carole said she'd like to write a book about my adoption and all the craziness involved, I was flattered. It was something we were doing together, and I enjoyed the closeness I felt when I shared my stories with her.

I knew there'd be a lot of information to cover, and it was hard sometimes to stay focused. Thankfully I had a great memory, and so I was able to give ages, and dates; which totally blew Carole's mind that I could remember so much. I looked forward to the afternoons she'd visit, and we'd discuss my story. My body might have been deteriorating, but my mind was like that of a twenty-year-old. I could remember even small details that surprised Carole.

I wasn't sure if I'd ever get to read the completed book, but even if I wasn't able to, I knew Carole would write it with all the sensitivity it required. I also knew she'd write it in my voice the best way she could. After all, it was my story, as Carole reminded me several times.

I didn't want anyone who read it to think I was angry about the things that happened to me. I'd forgiven them all. I had to. I couldn't carry that baggage around any longer. It doesn't mean I didn't still remember things. Carole would tell me I was like an elephant. I wouldn't forget anything. I could forgive, but forgetting; that was another thing.

IT WAS A BEAUTIFUL DAY, and although spring had not officially come it was pleasant enough to take a stroll around the grounds and visit the rose garden. Carole tenderly covered my legs with a lightweight cover and made sure I put on my sun visor. She packed a few essentials in my carry bag and strapped it to my wheelchair and off we went. I loved going outside, and Carole made sure I got out as much as possible. She pushed my wheelchair slowly avoiding the speed bumps in the parking area of my apartment building. She found the sidewalk and up and away we went. Soon we were rolling and talking. I don't know if I ever told her pointedly how much I enjoyed this, but I think she knew.

We ended up at the rose garden. It's where we usually went. It was there or the common area of the building so we could look at the tropical fish. It's funny, but back just a year or so I would have told you how boring that all sounded—visiting rose gardens and staring at tropical fish, but somehow it works when you're eighty-six and dependent on others.

I don't have any regrets, though. As difficult as life may have been, finding Charles more than made up for it, and the family we made was icing on the cake. My life was pretty ordinary once I met Charles. Well not really. Having your own private investigator's agency spiced things up considerably.

We worked as a team finding bad guys and the occasional unfaithful wife or husband—or runaway daughter. Life was fascinating and challenging in different ways, but we were doing it together.

What were the chances of me, with my background, getting a job at a private investigation firm, falling in love with the top investigator, and him helping me find out some of the answers to my questions? I'd say pretty slim, but that's just the way it happened.

For me to share my story, I have to start from the very beginning. As much as I tried to deny it, it shaped me. It made me who I am. And it starts right here.

IOWA DISTRICT COURT OF WOODBURY COUNTY

· · ·

OFFICE of

COLLEEN LEE MOLSKOW 101 COURT HOUSE

Clerk of District Court SIOUX CITY, IOWA

DEAR MRS. PHILLIPS:

We are unable to locate the birth record you have requested.

WE SUGGEST that you write to the State Office:

IOWA STATE DEPARTMENT OF HEALTH

Division of Vital Statistics

Des Moines, Iowa 50319

$4.00 EACH CERTIFICATE.

Yours Truly,

Clerk of District Court

Record Room

TIES THAT BIND

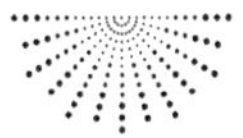

I WAS SHAKING, tears streaming down my face. I'd had a nightmare. I didn't have many of them, but this one was a doozy. Carole took me by the hand, "Mom. I'm here. It looks like you've had a bad dream. What was it about?"

Wiping the tears from my face, I shrugged. "Irma."

"Irma?" She repeated.

I nodded.

Caroled hugged me for a long minute and then pulled away and locked eyes with me. "Do you mind if I write the details of your dream down? It might be pertinent later on for the book."

I nodded. "Of course, I'm delighted you've taken such an interest in writing my story. Although I don't know how many people will find it interesting," I said laughing.

Carole reached out and took my hand into hers. "It doesn't matter what anyone else thinks. I'm doing this for us." She leaned over and kissed me lightly on the cheek.

I had a lot to be thankful for. Despite a somewhat traumatic beginning, I can honestly say, my life was better for having endured all the difficult times of my childhood.

I often wondered if it was a mere coincidence I was drawn to Charles or was it part of some larger design. What are the odds of being adopted, moving to California, landing a job at a private investigation firm, and later marrying the best PI west of the Mississippi?

"I'm sorry dear, I struggled for so many years with not knowing who I was. It still haunts me from time to time." She nodded and smiled. "Your dad was so great about putting up with all the neurotic behavior about my past. I pretended, at first, that I didn't care. I did that for a long time. But gradually, it became all I could think about. He became determined to help me find answers," I said, a tear forming on my bottom lid.

"Mom—"

"Let me finish, dear. What I was going to say was you all are the most important thing in my life. Your dad would have been so proud of how you all have stepped up and taken care of your old Ma."

"Mom, we'd all do it again," she said leaning over and kissing me lightly on the forehead. "I still want to talk to you about all those years and write it all down. Let's get the complete story into book form that we can all keep and cherish as a memorial to how you persevered and triumphed over a bad start in life. But, for now, let's stop talking about it. Let's go look at the roses."

ADOPTION WAS DONE DIFFERENTLY BACK THEN. Babies were often adopted with a handshake, not the mounds of red tape that it takes nowadays. I guess I should be thankful that loving parents found me—although that description is a bit of a stretch.

My dad showed me love and kindness. Mom, on the other hand, was not very warm or kind, and occasionally could be physically abusive. She always seemed to be irritated with me.

When I was old enough to read, I was handed a newspaper clipping about my entry into the family. The clipping said I was found lying on a bed and was estimated to be about nine months old. I tried to visualize the look on their faces when they saw this bundle of unexpected joy. I also wondered how on earth a nine-month-old stayed still on a strange bed, in a strange house. It wasn't until years later that I found my first real clue that maybe Mother wasn't telling the whole truth.

I had a half-sister, Teresa, from my dads' first marriage—at least, that's what they said. She didn't like me all that much either. She was about sixteen years older than me, and for the longest time, I wondered if she could be my real mom, and the half-sister story was just a cover. The animosity she showed me intensified over the years.

My earliest memories were of my years in Iowa. My dad owned a pool hall, and on many nights, I'd find myself among the adults watching them shoot pool, playing cards and throwing back cold ones. I never thought anything of it. It was normal as far as I knew.

We were a lively bunch. On Friday nights, the family would get together in our pool hall and party the night away. I distinctly remember that many nights, when I was about four years old, I would walk out the back door, climb the steps to our apartment over the pool hall, and put myself to bed. Looking back, I don't think anyone missed me.

I had a couple of aunts and uncles who adored me. They'd fuss over me and take me shopping, and we'd always end up at the ice-cream parlor. I always felt special when I was around them. If it weren't for them and my dad, life would have been pretty pathetic.

I had a couple of cousins, too. One, in particular, nicknamed Whitey, was more like an older brother. We rode bikes and played stickball in the street together along with the neighborhood kids.

It was during one of our playtimes that he spilled the beans about my real mother.

I ran home crying. Daddy was angry with Whitey for upsetting me.

Pulling him up by his suspenders, Daddy gave him a stern look. "Look here, Whitey. You don't know what you're talking about. Don't you ever say those ugly things to Patsy again," he said.

I still didn't know what the word meant, but I had a feeling that the word spewed from his mouth wasn't a good word.

When the Great Depression hit, we lost everything. The pool hall my dad just loved, the apartment overhead, and we would have lost the car too if it hadn't been for Daddy's sister. She saved the day by making all the late payments, with the stipulation we'd move to California.

My aunts and uncles had already made the trek out to California, so we packed up the car with the few possessions we still had, and off to sunny California, we went.

THE GREAT DEPRESSION hit all the states, but California had a few programs that allowed the men to earn a little stipend by doing work for the CCC (California Conservation Corps). We moved into what would be considered the projects by today's standards. I started school—which I dearly loved, and we settled into California life easily.

Food was scarce. We received vouchers equivalent to food stamps to get certain foods such as cheese and bread. We were surrounded by acres of orchards of apples, peaches, and avocados. It was a natural food pantry right in our backyard. However, when fruit was the only choice to stop a growling stomach, you got tired of the taste and texture. I vowed that when I earned my own money, I'd buy cookies and cakes and never eat fruit again. Everyone in my family will tell you I have a sweet tooth. Just look in my dresser drawer, and you'll find bags of Hershey's Kisses.

Food wasn't the only thing that was scarce. Money

was non-existent, but we had each other for company and entertainment. Whitey would sometimes bring over his guitar, and he and I would put on little skits and entertain the neighborhood, parents and all. I recall one such memory that involved singing a duet called Little Sir Echo. It was a popular song of the times, and to this day, I can recite the words.

After we had finished our performance, a few adults told us we should enter a local talent show that was being advertised.

I wasn't the least bit nervous performing on the stage in front of so many people. I was a natural, they said. It wasn't too much of a surprise that we'd won the grand prize - a plastic trophy, and a free ice-cream cone.

It was great to see Daddy, my aunts; Toots, Margie, and Annie in the audience. Mother was there too, but as usual, no smile, no reaction whatsoever. Thinking back, I don't think she even clapped for us.

Daddy rushed toward us, a broad smile plastered all over his face. Mother was by his side, but only a slight smirk emerged on hers. "You were so good. You should take your act on the road," he said.

I had a few friends, but my closest friend was Shirley. We met at school. She didn't live in the low-income apartments; her parents had a beautiful house in an excellent part of town. She would invite me over to play, and I was so in awe of her. She had her bedroom full of things that I could only dream of having. Her family was very kind to me, and I found myself not wanting to go home.

With her hands on her hips, Mother said in a disgusted voice, "You sure spend a lot of time over at Shirley's."

WE'D GIVEN up the severe winters of Iowa for sunny skies and warmer temperatures. It seemed like a good exchange. Life was hard, though, especially after Daddy got ill. I was just a young girl, but even then, the word cancer was scary. He tried to remain positive, even though our situation was anything but that.

I didn't realize just how sick he was until he was on his deathbed. Mother had the priest visit, and he performed last rites. Then the realization hit me and hit me hard. I ran out of the room crying. Life would never be the same. I knew that much.

Daddy died when I was about twelve. We didn't know a lot about cancer then. I just knew that one day he was fine, the next he was sick, and then he died. It happened so fast. At least, that's the way I remembered it. It was one of the saddest days of my life. I lost the only ally I had in the house.

When Daddy was alive, he acted as a buffer between mother and me. After he passed, my buffer was gone. Until I could stand up for myself, I would endure even more ponytail or arm yanking and a lot of yelling.

Mother drank occasionally, and it was after she'd had a few too many she made the revelation, "If only he'd kept his thing in his pants, you'd never been born." One could take this statement one of two ways, but she was letting me know she wasn't pleased being saddled with the outcome of Daddy's sexual exploits. I thought about that statement a lot, but it would be years before it meant anything concrete to me.

I kept to myself and planned my getaway. When I turned sixteen, I left home. It was the best thing I ever did. Living with Mother was too difficult. I reminded her of a part of her past she didn't want to remember. I didn't know what it was, but I could sense it within every fiber of me. She didn't even try to stop me. In fact, she held the door open for me as I left.

After I had left home, my half-sister Teresa and Mother moved back to Iowa. I was glad, as I didn't want to run into them. They'd made my life difficult enough. I wasn't stupid. After Daddy died, I could sense they felt I was more of a burden than a family member. I was happier without them in my life.

SHIRLEY'S FAMILY offered to let me live with them until I could save up enough money to live on my own. Shirley and I had plans to share a place together anyway, after graduation. Of course, plans don't always end as you hoped they would.

I knew that I needed to earn money, so I dropped out of high school and enrolled in secretarial school. Back then, you didn't have to have a high school diploma to enroll.

I learned how to type, take shorthand, and various other secretarial duties. I was ready for the workforce.

I held various jobs around the city where I used my newly learned skills. I was a good employee. I was prompt, courteous, and willing to learn new things.

Shirley and I had many fun and carefree days at the beach. Young and dumb, we both almost fell for a sailor or two. They were everywhere. Long Beach was a major port for the Navy.

Shirley and I had big dreams and settling down wasn't one of them—for that moment, anyway. So, after a few close calls with marriage proposals, Shirley and I decided it was time to leave her parent's house. Our first place was a small apartment over a mechanic's garage. It probably wasn't the smartest thing we'd ever done. Young men were constantly working on cars there. The wolf whistles and catcalls became more than a nuisance.

Shirley shot the grease monkeys a dirty look. "What are you looking at?" She said as she stormed up the steps to our apartment.

I saw it all from the window. Slamming it shut to let them know I didn't appreciate them upsetting my best friend, I waited for Shirley to enter the apartment. Seeing the look of disgust on her face, I offered a calming voice. "Those creeps don't mean any harm. They can't help themselves." I winked at her.

Shirley let out a sigh. "It may be time for us to look for a new place."

I started scouring the newspapers for something in a family-friendly environment.

"This sounds perfect, Shirley; a one bedroom flat near the beach."

"How much?" She asked as she pulled the paper out of my hands.

"Let's take a look at it. Maybe we can get second jobs to help pay for it?" I said reaching for the phone.

Those were the days. Shirley and I were like most

young women of that generation. We worked hard, but we also played hard. We could be found on many a Saturday night at the local club dancing the night away. And, because of our close proximity to Hollywood, Shirley and I would venture into town to see if we'd run into any famous stars... and we did. I recall seeing Clark Gable, and Rita Hayworth. Back then, stars were more humble, down to earth. They waved, spoke to us and then went about their business. We were thrilled, of course, as we were just nobodies trying to make it in the big, bad world.

Shirley and I stood holding each other. We trembled when she looked our way. I shrieked. "Oh. My. God. Look. It's Rita Hayworth."

Rita looked our way and then shot us the most beautiful smile. We both smiled back. She walked up to the roped off area we were standing behind, and gently took our autograph book out of our hands.

Shirley looked at me and hugged me. "Thank you, Miss Hayworth," we both said at the same time.

Like most young people, I struggled with paying the rent. I had no help from anyone in my family, but Shirley came from a well to do family, and she seemed to never be out of money.

I realized I needed a better job than the one I currently held at the local insurance company, and began my search. And that's how I landed the job at Phillips Private Investigation Firm and went to work for Charles Phillips. I needed the extra money to pay for that gorgeous flat, one block away from the beach.

It's funny how you remember things. Years later, we'd travel to the area where the gorgeous one bedroom flat was located. It was anything but. However, everyone who was someone wanted to live within walking distance to the beach. We were no different.

ABOUT THE AUTHOR

A USA Today bestselling author, Debbie writes sweet contemporary romance and women's fiction. She lives in South Carolina with her husband and two dachshund rescues, Dash and Briar. She loves to hike, work in the garden, and on most sunny days, you can find her enjoying her backyard. She's an avid supporter of animal rescue, and as such, pledges to happily donate a percentage of all book sales to local and national rescue organizations. When you purchase any of her books, you're also helping animals.

To find out more about Debbie, check out her website at www.authordebbiewhite.com